ALEXANDER GEORGIADES THE SPYMASTER THAT ENDED WWII

Translated from Greek by the author

Photini Tomai

Pharos Books

ISBN: 978-93-5546-374-6
eISBN: 978-93-5546-375-3

©Publisher

Publisher: Pharos Books (P) Ltd.
Plot No.-55, Main Mother Dairy Road
Pandav Nagar, East Delhi-110092
Phone: 011-40395855, +14049995474
WhatsApp: +91 8368220032
E-mail: sales@pharosbooks.in
Website: www.pharosbooks.in
First Edition: 2022

ALEXANDER GEORGIADES
THE SPYMASTER THAT ENDED WWII
Photini Tomai

CONTENTS

Historical Brief

Greece was the only country in Europe to suffer a triple foreign occupation by the Axis Forces: the Italian control zone included two-thirds of Greek territory which passed into German control after the Italian capitulation in September 1943; the areas of Eastern Macedonia and Western Thrace were granted to the Bulgarian occupation army, except for the border zone with Turkey, which was held by German forces; over the remaining territory of Greece, Germany maintained control.

Relative to its size and population, Greece suffered the heaviest losses of all occupied European countries: approximately 15,000 officers and soldiers were lost on the Albanian front; over 880,000 civilians died from hunger and hardship; 86 percent of its Jewish population was exterminated during the Holocaust; one million were left homeless and two million survived, thanks to international food aid. The occupation forces destroyed 9,000 villages and towns, virtually the entire road and rail network and 52 crucial central bridges. The vast majority of Greece's merchant fleet was eliminated and a vast number of archaeological treasures were looted through illegal excavations and thefts from museums.

Minimal reparations were received after the war. It was aid provided via the Marshall Plan that helped the country rebuild its economy and stand on its feet again.

After the German and Bulgarian forces withdrew, the country continued to suffer immense losses, both in lives and material damage, during the civil war that broke out between the conservative forces and the British, on the one side and on the other the forces of the Democratic Army.

Essentially, the Greek conflict had begun much earlier, when the first clashes between the resistance groups broke out in the summer of 1943. The second round commenced in Eastern Macedonia on December 1, 1944, and became more severe in Athens two days later. It was followed by a lengthy period of mutual retaliation, often termed "white terrorism." The period between September 1946 and September 1949 was the third and most bloody round followed by the defeat of the Democratic Army and the outflow of a large segment of Greece's population toward countries of the former Eastern Bloc. The losses suffered by the country proved to be enormous.

Author's Introductory Note

The writing of this book stems from the author's obligation to the memory of Alexander Georgiades, a brave Greek-American from the isle of Karpathos who in 1942, at the age of 42, entered the ranks of the OSS.

Alex Martin Georgiades, as he was naturalized in the USA, came from hardscrabble stock: the son of a teacher and grandson of a priest from the village of Othos, Karpathos. He left the island as the Dodecanese passed from Ottoman to Italian hands and arrived in Athens in order to finish High School. There, he lived as the house guest of his cousin, then a Ministry of Defense typist. Afterwards, seeking to better his lot in life, he emigrated to America. He studied electrical engineering at the Carnegie Institute, Pittsburgh, and opened a small lighting business in the same city. There, he was recruited by agents of the FBI and entered the ranks of the U.S. Office of Strategic Services, the OSS.

Until the establishment of the OSS, the United States did not possess an overseas intelligence service. President Franklin D. Roosevelt took the decision to found the service when America entered the Second World War. To head this new service, Roosevelt appointed his former Columbia Law School classmate, General William J. Donovan, a millionaire lawyer of Irish descent, also known as "Wild Bill" due to the courage and resolve he had shown as a World War I officer, for which he had been awarded the Congressional Medal of Honor.

Georgiades, along with a few thousand other young people from European countries now in the American army who had been recruited because of their knowledge of their mother tongues, was sent to Cairo after intensive military training at camps in Florida and Washington. From there, equipped with a special Greek passport issued by the government-in-exile of Emmanuel Tsouderos, Georgiades was accredited as an interpreter at the Greek consulate in Adrianople (or Edirne). Using his official status and the Turkish city as a base and border town with Greece, he was active in the OSS Secret Intelligence branch (SI), penetrating the Greek interior via the Evros, as well as Bulgaria, and preparing the ground for acts of sabotage against the Axis Powers as part of an Allied operation code-named "Noah's Ark." Without his ingenuity and bravery, defying fear and risking his life in a series of dangerous missions against advanced enemy positions, there would-be no-good end to the mission of the team led by another Greek-American OSS officer of the Special Operations branch (SO), James Kellis, who blew up bridges at Svilengrad and Alexandroupolis in June 1944.

The winds of victory from those successes of the Americans, who emerged as redeemers of the Greeks, had so instilled the people of Evros with courage and confidence that they united with the insurgents in joint incitements against the enemy. Young and old — even women and children — used shovels, axes and any other implement they could find to drive the Germans from their vicinity to the deadly battles of Orestiada, Didymoteichon and Soufli.

Thus, Evros became the first region in Greece which felt the sweet joy of liberty and Georgiades, so beloved by the locals, was decorated after his return to America withthe Bronze Star of the U.S. Army, having endured the bloody "Dekemvriana" conflicts in Athens in the immediate postwar period. During the war, he had received the distinction of the Legion of Merit for uncovering a network of German double agents within Turkey. Uncorroborated information notes that for decades afterwards and until the early 1980s a school of Orestiada was named in honor of "Alekos Georgiades." Elderly inhabitants of the city still harbor vivid memories of Georgiades and his actions to this day.

All the same, he was scorned by the British and British Intelligence because in his frequent and comprehensive reports to the American government, he was unflagging in denouncing the factious role the British played for months against the Greek people, by supplying arms to the monarchist-fascists and collaborators of the Bulgarian guerrillas of Tsaus Anton (Antonios Fosteridis) who wanted to eliminate the fighters of ELAS (the National Popular Liberation Army), the only ones who were actually fighting the Axis Forces.

It is a fact that during this period the American government's, and President Roosevelt's, policy on the Balkans and on Greece in particular was diametrically opposed to that of the British. For the Americans, the war itself was top priority, whereas the British and Churchill put greater weight on postwar political considerations. With Roosevelt's unquestioning trust, Donovan's role had a catalytic effect. It was Donovan who, through the Allied Headquarters in Cairo, instructed Georgiades to join forces with ELAS. Characteristically, Donovan often told his interlocutors that he would not oppose placing even Stalin himself on the OSS payroll if by so doing he could secure his participation in Hitler's defeat.

Even though Georgiades followed faithfully the American government's orders and cooperated with EAM (National Liberation Front) and ELAS, he was later denounced as a Communist and experienced the harsh ordeals of McCarthyism. Another impacting factor was that Georgiades, unlike others, refused to join the ranks of the CIA after the OSS was dissolved at the end of the war.

For reasons such as these, he remained in obscurity for decades. It was not until the 1980s that his role was spotlighted in a presentation made at a meeting of the Modern Greek Studies Association by the Byzantinist — and later on a deputy minister in the government of George Papandreou — the late Angelica Laiou, who passed away prematurely.

The question she raised at the MGSA conference was whether there was material on this brave and resourceful Greek-American hero in the archives of the Ministry of Foreign Affairs. I took this as a challenge and found numerous references on Georgiades' activities in six files from the period.

An interview I gave to Greek television that was seen by Georgiades' relatives in Pittsburgh resulted in direct contact with his nephew, Mike Epitropoulos, a professor of Sociology at the University of Pittsburgh, who supplied handwritten notes by Georgiades and copies from the National Archives and Records Administration (NARA) and the CIA library at Lexington, files which Laiou also studied.

Warm thanks are expressed to Georgiades' family, in particular his son Peter, who practices law in Pittsburgh. Of the three children — the eldest, Thalia, who is an artist and lives still in San Diego, and the youngest, Aristotle, an economist who lives in Washington — it is Peter, with his cousin Mike, who helped in the writing of this book by overseeing its development and by making sure that the historical truth comes through as reliably as possible.

Traveling to Pittsburgh, I was able, with facilitation by the family, to visit the site of Georgiades' pre-war commercial enterprise as well as his post-war residence on a small farm, where Cold War raids by FBI agents sought in vain evidence that might connect him with the then Soviet Union.

I would like to express my gratitude to colleagues who, over the years, shared my anxieties as well as my surprises — including the discovery that eminent American archaeology professors, with whom I participated in excavations, were also OSS officers during the war — and in my delight at continually finding new information on my "hero," as I now refer to him with legitimate familiarity and affection.

Life in my homeland, Karpathos

I was born on a cold day in March 1898 in Othos, the highest village on the island of Karpathos. It was at dawn on a Monday and I was to be the youngest among my siblings — Marigo, my sister, and Nikos, my brother, who was the first of us to die. My mother's name was Varvaroula. She lived well into her old age, remained strong and worked all the days of the year without exception. My father, George, was a teacher and judge on the island. My grandfather, Stamatis, was a priest. He was beloved and everyone showed him great respect, as was also the case with my father. I was taught by both to love my homeland and to serve all the values that honor man and exalt humanity on higher spheres of morality and justice.

Although I left my island when I was only fourteen years old to enroll at the Rigopoulos Commercial School of Athens, images of my birthplace never left my heart — neither during difficult years while living abroad, nor during wartime when I found myself in Greece again. The whitewashed houses and little streets bathed in light by the pitiless Aegean sun, the flower-packed courtyards and the aroma of crusty bread that filled the air from the outdoor home ovens — these, individually and combined, formed the womb of my birth. The blue-green waters that gently lap against the pebbly beaches of my island in temperate months, but in wintertime, with raging winds, beat the shoreline and change color as if in mourning — these, too, are part of my memories. My favorite snack was cold watermelon and bread. With a slice in each hand, I would run headlong downhill through the village to find my friends, with whom I shared endless hours of play every day. I was a skinny but strong child, and this helped me through the difficult wartime years.

When I was born, Karpathos and the islands of the Dodecanese were possessions of the Ottoman Empire. Even so, we were raised as authentic Greeks and enjoyed the benefits of the Ottoman administrative system. Because Karpathos was the poorest island of all, we paid no taxes, by edict of the Sultan, except for the well-known head tax and something minor for the land each family occupied. All of their taxes were collected by the mayor and sent to the governor's seat in Rhodes. Similarly, men did not enter the army and generally there was an organized system of a fully collective and democratic public life, something comparable to the people's democracy, or *laokratia*, that I would come to know decades later, as applied by EAM under those difficult conditions of guerrilla war in Evros.

In the event of very important news, it was the responsibility of the mayor to tell the priest and then for him to announce it after the end of Sunday's liturgy. For emergencies, we had the town crier and we, the children of the island, had great fun following him and repeating out loud what he said.

The mayor and village elders were elected annually. One individual from each family voted and he was their leader. The villages were divided into geographic regions and the assembly of mayors for each district, after determining total taxes levied, apportioned the amounts by village and by family. Any disputes or violations of the law were discussed by the mayor and village elders in an open gathering in the presence of all the villagers, usually following Sunday service. All domestic and property issues, on the other hand, were resolved by the so-called religious courts, which consisted of three members elected from the all-municipal magistrate assembly, headed by the bishop.

In all matters of our community life, the Turks kept a distance, except, for instance, murder which involved a Turkish judge, or *kaymakam*, assisted by three *antazathes* or local Karpathian judges appointed by the Rhodes governor every two or four years, though I am not any more sure of the details. The Turkish judge had the services of a police guard and a translator, usually Greek, since the entire procedure was conducted in Greek.

In the system of absolute autonomy which we enjoyed, the schools of the island functioned and followed the educational programs of liberated Greece, without any involvement by the Ottomans, proof of which was the fact that the Greek history lessons contained many chapters that cast the Turks in a very negative light.

Each village voted for its own superintendent of education and schoolmasters were paid from the taxes that the families paid. Religious tolerance remained a fundamental component and precept of Ottoman administration.

Characteristic selflessness distinguished the notables of our society; in point of fact, none of them received compensation for their services. Their participation in public affairs was purely an issue of honor. Indeed, there were instances where they had to cover treasury outlays themselves.

All the same, the political antagonisms which have always characterized Greek society were not absent. In Karpathos, we had two parties and, while it might seem odd, I again encountered this potent bipartisan system here in America with the Democratic and Republican parties. On my island the first, the progressives, let us say, were called "The Unshod," whereas the second, who were the conservatives, were known as "The Well-Shod." Every village had backers of both factions.

In our village, the eminent "Unshod" was my father because he had been a teacher and mayor for over fifteen years. He was the first qualified graduate on the island (in the absence of educators, this role was mercifully undertaken by priests) and, moreover, he had been elected member of the religious court for two or three terms.

The period of Ottoman rule was followed by that of the Italians when in 1912, after the Italo-Turkish War, the Dodecanese were granted to Italy. Italian sovereignty began with disastrous consequences for the Greek population, who literally suffered at their hands. I still recall the distress and sorrow on the faces of the adults as they glimpsed the gray and, to my young eyes, tremendous Italian warship. The Italian officer and his retinue stepped ashore to announce that, blockaded by their fleet, our islands now belonged to Italy.

As though it were only yesterday, I recall the sudden silence that prevailed. No one spoke. There were only sideways glances between us. The air itself stood still. Not a sound was to be heard. Everything seemed to become glacial.

Turning their backs on this scene, my fellow countrymen began to depart one by one, as if in unspoken agreement. So did my father, whose hand was affectionately upon my shoulder. I could nearly read his thoughts. And from that instant an image haunted me: the time I would be on a ship leaving my island. There appeared to be no future for anyone here, not on these shores in the middle of the Aegean Sea....

Although still a juvenile, I was not mistaken. The measures imposed by the Italians — which in numerous instances was almost a process of cruel de-hellenization, the goal of which was the Italianization of the local population — were unprecedented at the time and cost many of my compatriots' lives, who I never ceased to defend here in America as an active member of the Dodecanese Youth.

My love of my homeland kept me unbent and unbowed when confronting life's difficulties. I owe much to my father and my two grandfathers, who each influenced me differently on the course I chose to carve out later in life.

These three men were of a wholly different character and each had his share in shaping my own. And it is salient that, in early adolescence, I could discern such differences, understand them and compare them without repudiating any of the three. One of these was — what else? — religion. I became an altar-boy to my maternal grandfather, a priest, who was widely known on the island as "Papa Sakellis" and lived exactly next door to us. I followed him everywhere. In church services at the holy altar and later with the title of "lector," I was a mere step away from entering the priesthood myself.

My father's views were completely different. After his graduation in Athens, he returned to the island and, initially, opened a café. I never learned who converted him to Freemasonry. In that era, for someone to affirm as a Mason was tantamount to proclaiming themselves a nonbeliever, which is why my grandfather called him "the Antichrist."

My other grandfather, from my father's side, was a quiet and even-tempered man who, with great patience, taught me grammar and Greek history. This tranquil man's influence on my character seems to have left no serious traces for anyone witnessing my subsequent career of daring and steadfast courage in the face of insurmountable difficulties, as confirmed also by my superior officers in the US Army.

To his credit, my father never attempted to prevent or even preclude the influences of my sacerdotal grandfather. He did, however, allow me to read the philosophy books he brought with him from Athens. While I might not have understood much then, seeds of skepticism began to grow within me and my close relationship with religion concluded somewhere there.

One event that marked me and contributed to my turnaround occurred when some of my father's friends gathered at our home one evening for a glass of wine. Among them was my uncle, the priest's son. Somehow or other, at one point the conversation turned to a wooden holy crucifix that my grandfather possessed. It was said that whoever had this crucifix in their possession would not be touched even by a bullet. My father disputed this belief. My uncle answered back and, broadly speaking, tempers began to rise until it was decided to conduct an experiment with a rooster from our chicken coop. They secured the crucifix around the rooster's neck, propped him up against a wall and shot him. The result: the cockerel paid dearest of all. The incident developed into a grand scandal which was heard from one end of the island to the other and, in any event, established my father as Antichrist and extracted me from the sphere of metaphysics once and for all.

All the experiences which I lived through, from an early age and onward, shaped my worldview concerning life. And so if someone asked about my perspective on things in general and my political persuasions, I would unhesitatingly reply that my sentiments were clearly progressive and Left-leaning — but a democratic non-dogmatic Left and certainly far removed from partisan orientations of any sort.

I was already eighteen years old when I made the big decision to depart for America. During those years, such travel was neither leisurely nor uncomplicated. The journey itself took nearly a month. However, I was determined not to let that get in the way of my plans. Life itself had shown me the way. Moreover, in no other country was one able to truly live free and follow the path of one's own choosing. There alone. I wanted to study, to become somebody and to make my family proud.

In Search of a Better Life in Pittsburgh

Late on the morning of January 13, 1916, the ocean liner "Themistocles" entered the port of Patras. This huge ship, which flew our merchant marine Greek flag, had been built in Scotland just over a decade earlier. The ship now sailed on the New York – Patras route. On that Thursday morning, I boarded the "Themistocles" along with about one hundred other nomads. All of them were, like myself, traveling third class. The ship's passenger capacity was roughly one thousand seven hundred, but we were probably no more than four hundred, including the thirty-five or so first- and second-class passengers. Among them were two Jewish students from Smyrna, but I could not speak with them, since passengers from economy were not allowed to roam about in other areas of the ship.

The trip was unpleasant because of its duration, combined with the ugly dead-of-winter weather. Also, even though Greece had not yet entered the war, there were fears of potential misadventure because of hostile activity. Everyone could remember what had happened on that black Friday nearly a year before, on May 7, 1915, when the Germans torpedoed the RMS "Lusitania" off the coast of Ireland, at a loss of two thousand lives.

After about a month at sea, we entered New York harbor on Saturday, February 5. Even at a distance, the Statue of Liberty seemed to stand out in the fog. My heart danced madly, as if it were about to break. I was in a state of emotional upheaval, but I was also afraid of the unknown.

Fear is a prodigious word. Still, it does not fully describe what I felt. Disquiet would be a better fit, especially since I never in my life felt fear. Not ever. Not even later when I heard bullets whizzing around me while on the mountains or in the "Dekemvriana" conflicts in Athens…

We disembarked, in an orderly grouping, on a small island set up for receiving foreigners, known as Ellis Island. Though ambivalent about the unknown, we were without a hint of impatience.

It was bitter cold and snowing. The wooden reception room was so humid that the two or three large hearths made little difference.

One by one, we passed through the checks. Someone switched my country of origin and wrote "Turkey" instead of "Greece." News arrives late here, I thought, since they apparently had not yet learned about the Italians.

I declared myself to be a student and remained with twenty others in third class, awaiting both an examination by a physician and an interview.

The official who interviewed me was named Foster. I still remember his name. It must have been he who changed my papers from "student" to "employee" allowing me to set foot on American soil, since as a "student" I would need someone to guarantee for my stay and my studies.

His name highlighted in the list of alien passengers for the United States immigration officer at Ellis Island.

I remained on Ellis Island for one day. On the following Sunday, at around 11 in the morning, I was formally allowed to set foot in America.

Here I was at last. In America. I thought I might be dreaming and squeezed one hand with the other to make sure I was awake.

My adjustment to America was not effortless. I had left behind a life without an excess of material goods, though I had lived in an environment of security and love. Here, however, besides my eldest brother, Nikos, who I had not seen since I was five years old, and who had settled and lived as an immigrant in Bridgeville since 1902, I was alone.

Nikos was in the confectionery business and had opened a small ice cream parlor. I did not wish to become a burden on him and instead sought to figure out my own life. I knew precisely what I wanted to do:

I had no doubts that I wanted to study, but the priorities now were to survive and to ensure food and board. We formed a group with friends I had met just after arriving. We shared whatever information came our way about job opportunities.

Folly and foolishness were no strangers to our youth. I still recall with a laugh that day when, while walking in a park in Cleveland, someone ahead of us bent down to pick up a wallet. When he showed it to us, it was stuffed with dollars. We thought how unlucky we were that we had not seen it first, but he seemed oddly willing to share with us this treasure that had fallen into his hands. He recommended we put into a paper sack, along with the wallet, whatever coins we had in our pockets and afterwards, he suggested, we would divvy it all up. None of us objected. After all, we were three and he was but one. He then asked that we wait, while he dashed off to a nearby shop before we divided the lot. It must have been laughable for someone to see us waiting for about nearly an hour. In the end, we decided the stranger would not return and, still holding the unopened sack, we left.

We went into the first Greek restaurant we came across. We were famished and thinking we now had loads of cash all to ourselves, ordered whatever our hearts desired. When the time came to settle our bill, we opened the paper sack only to discover that, instead of money, the wallet was stuffed with paper, whereas among us we had only my four dollars and some change. The other lad, who spoke better English and facilitated our discussions, had another sixteen.

We went slack-jawed. Ashen-faced, we apologized to the proprietor, gave him our friend's sixteen dollars and exited. Humiliated and conscience-stricken, we went to a nearby coffee shop to discuss the idea of heading to Warren, Ohio, near Cleveland, in order to look for work in the steel industry.

My two friends already knew the job and, since we did not have enough for all of us to travel there, I stayed behind to await their news of whether there was a position for me. It was funny that we behaved like cowboys seeking their fortune in the West, inspired by our favorite Western movie hero of the era, William S. Hart.

I remained on my own to contemplate what to do: a stranger in a city where I knew no one. At an adjacent table sat a kindly man. He was Greek and from his pronunciation I understood he was a Cretan. We struck up a conversation and he asked where I was from and what work I did. I told him the story of how I found myself there and he quickly put me at ease. He even offered to host me. His nephew, who was the same age as I was, lived with him. On the following day, the three of us set off in search of work. They took me to a Greek patisserie and somehow along the way my cowboy adventure ended.

My Life in Pittsburgh

When I first set foot in Pittsburgh, it was a paradise for immigrants. This was perhaps why James Barton, the eminent biographer of his day, himself an immigrant who settled in Pennsylvania after graduating from university in New York, had compared the city to an uncovered cauldron of perdition. Immigrants flocked to the city: French Quebecois, Irish, Italians and Greeks mainly from the islands still under Ottoman occupation. There were even Afro-Americans from the agrarian regions of southern America. Collectively, they formed a mosaic of ethnicities, each of which claimed its own rights. Most workers labored in the mines and the glass and steel industries. In the 1940s, with the outbreak of war, production was revved up to a 24-hour basis, yielding roughly 95 million tons of steel for the Allied war machine. More than a thousand such factories existed in the region when I arrived there. In the year I was born, a great man, Andrew Carnegie — who founded the Carnegie Institute of Technology which I attended — managed to buy small production facilities and turn them into an economic colossus, transforming Pittsburgh from a small city into the eighth largest American metropolis.

With four rivers running through it and multiple bridges uniting districts divided by water, it could be beautiful. But its polluted air that reeks of charcoal all over the city, combined with the humidity and the cold of an endless winter, gives it a gray and mournful ambiance. It constricts one's heart. My gaze — conditioned to meander the endless blue of the Aegean under unrelenting warmth of the sun, which made everything on my island, my heroic Karpathos, appear bleached — struggled to adapt here, in the city of what would eventually become my second homeland.

The America of my era seemed to foreigners much the same as it does today. It was the paradise of every poor soul, young or middle-aged, made desperate by the lingering economic malaise in Europe, where one sought a better life for oneself and one's family after having crossed the ocean in a wretched state to be greeted by the humbling checks and controls of Ellis Island. Thousands of souls were stacked like sacks in the damp chambers of temporary detention facilities, stoically waiting in interminable lines to open their mouths for American examiners, to cough and demonstrate they did not have tuberculosis, the disease that had decimated thousands of Europeans and might now pour across their new homeland.

Some already knew their destinations, as some relative or friend awaited them. Others, however, seemed entirely lost, not knowing anything, not even the rudiments of language, and were unable to communicate. A veritable Babel of individuals of all origins with religion as their common ground, given that the majority were Catholics. We Orthodox were a minority but united among ourselves, as was evident during Sunday services when we congregated in churches to exchange information of all kinds interspersed with news from home. For the most part, the news we shared was about employment, since only a few were able to access the press.

Compared with the larger and literally hopeless mass of immigrants, I found myself in a much better position. For one thing, I knew a bit of English. For another, there was the security of my brother Nikos, who had arrived in Ohio as an immigrant a decade before. This was a good beginning for a youth such as myself. And I could undertake all sorts of prospective short-term jobs in order to survive — not only to avoid burdening Nikos, I was indeed keen on my goal of studying and creating better prospects for my future.

Creating a family did not cross my mind for a moment. I had no idea if I would continue here forever or whether I would return to my island, if it was, of course, liberated. For me, my family remained my poverty-stricken parents, my sister Marigo and my elderly grandfathers. They were the ones I wished to aid and to make proud of my progress. I was determined that nothing would hinder me, even when I returned dirty and exhausted from the factory every afternoon to a frigid room, only four or five square meters, which I rented as my home.

Naturally, within a few months matters appeared to change for the better and my conditions of survival improved significantly, thanks to Ellen, an American lady, much older than me, who worked as an accountant in a company just outside the city. We met regularly at the grocery store in my neighborhood. She found my English amusing and in the beginning she offered to help me improve my language skills on the weekends. She lived alone in a small but well-kept apartment in the city center. We quickly fell in love with one another and decided to stay together. I found work in a commercial food enterprise with much better hours and income, my English improved to the point of not standing out and the sole item that betrayed my origin was my black hair — which was part of my charm, since the movie idol for women then was none other than the famous Rudolf Valentino.

The path toward university, which was the dream of my life, was now open. I had only to enroll in the first year at the School of Electrical Engineering of the Carnegie Institute of Technology, one of the most renowned institutes in America, founded by the well-known Scottish-American industrialist Andrew Carnegie.

America, however, was not what it is today and racism was rampant everywhere. It was African Americans who were mostly in the cross-hairs of white Americans, but so too were Jews as well as people from Southern Europe, such as Greeks and Italians. The same was true for the Irish, who were frequently victims of racial discrimination in the workplace. Social gatherings were inconceivable.

The truth is, I held down several jobs before I could enroll at Carnegie and the going was rough until I could begin working professionally on my subject. But I quickly found my rhythm. My job was installing neon signs, which were quite fashionable then, and I began closing one deal after another. I was convinced that the worst was behind me.

I cannot stress enough how difficult it was for foreigners in America then. If upon meeting compatriots in the street or in a train we were heard speaking Greek, the refrain was always the same: "Go back where you came from, filthy Greeks." Even the cleanest and loveliest Greek restaurant in all of Pittsburgh went by the disparaging name "The Dirty Spoon."

While at university, my Anglo-Saxon fellow students were friendly towards me, though none of them befriended me outside of school. That is precisely the predicament of Afro-Americans today. And if they happened to invite me to some party, one could clearly see that they behaved differently toward me, the foreigner, than among themselves — not to mention how they reacted when some girl seemed to be fascinated by my dark hair that was reminiscent of Valentino. Then, matters truly became bedeviling as those around me behaved much as they do today when they see an African-American out and about with a blonde girl. This prejudice against me left a bitterness which, regrettably, has not yet gone. Indeed, I confess that I struggle to free myself from this when I am obligated to consort with Anglo-Saxons, whom I try to avoid, preferring instead the company of Italians, Poles, Serbs and even Chinese.

I endured the worst, however, during the McCarthy period, when anti-communist hysteria became a movement against foreigners and many Greek businessmen saw their jobs destroyed. One result of such persecutions was the establishment of the American Hellenic Educational Progressive Association, known also as AHEPA, in order to protect the Greeks of America. When a branch was established in Pittsburgh, I became a member without second thought. We, the Greeks of America, needed to really struggle to stop being victims of prejudice and I must emphasize that a catalytic role was played by the Greek "OCHI/OXI" in response to the Italian arrogance of 1940. Only then did the climate begin to change: over the course of several days, the news reports praised Greece's robust defense against Italy's attack as a totally heroic act, presenting the Greeks almost as ancient demigods.

In the Years of the Great War

Just when my life finally seemed to acquire a normal pace — though in the meantime I had separated from Ellen who needed to move in with her parents in Philadelphia —, war broke out in Europe. The news arrived here almost like an avalanche. Europe was ablaze and the reverberation of Greece's heroic resistance, which everyone admired, made every Greek soul swell with pride.

Many people passed by my small lighting business to congratulate me and in the hope of learning more than what was on the news. When went to the market for my daily shopping, anyone aware of my ancestry would ask me without fail about my kith and kin. A century after the Greek Revolution, the philhellenic sensitivities of Americans had surfaced for the second time. The elderly among them recalled tales of their forefathers about support given for the independence struggles of a humbled Greece, when boatloads of food and clothing were sent from American ports, destined for starving women, children and the aged.

Although Pittsburgh was then a poor, working-class city, it managed to raise a thousand five hundred dollars in January 1827, all from the steel mill workers, for the needs of the Greek revolutionaries. Unlike the Italians, who are scorned more with each passing day, we Greeks, particularly after the defense at the Albanian front, had become sought after and entered the hearts and homes of our American friends and neighbors.

Then, something strange happened to me. Until that moment, I had never harbored hatred for any people. But now — perhaps because of the Italian occupation of the Dodecanese and its cruelty against ordinary people, who refused to abandon their language, religion or customs which they managed to preserve during four hundred years of Turkish subjugation, or because of the cowardly attack by Italy after Mussolini's ultimatum and the courageous "OXI" of our people — it was time to revise much of what I believed until then.

In those days, news from our families and friends on the island came to us in drips and drops. We learned, however, that, apart from hunger and material deprivations, they were all well. But the inhabitants of Karpathos had learned to live frugally, so they could persevere and live with even less during the war.

Those who lived in the large urban centers were the ones who endured the greatest famine. They had now been reduced to skeletal figures and would fall over dead in the middle of the streets while walking. Dozens of such photographs came into our hands and were published in newspapers and periodicals of the day. Particularly moving were the photographs of scrawny children with saucepans in their hands waiting in lines at soup kitchens, babies with their mouths cleaving to the desiccated bosoms of their mothers and other, older people, with empty stares, slack-jawed and sitting on sidewalks and building stoops, unable to stand on their own legs. Disheartening scenes of the impoverishment of a whole people who stubbornly resisted and organized with zero resources an army of young students and working-class people who sometimes fought in the mountains or in the occupied cities. The participation of women in that unequal struggle against the Italians and the Germans moved Americans, who put family above everything else and recognized the leading role of women and mothers.

My Enlistment in the US Army

In the midst of the climate of those days, and after two whole years of European bloodshed, I found myself a volunteer in the ranks of the American army. I had in fact attempted to enlist earlier, during the First World War, but because I had not yet received American citizenship and my papers declared me as a Turk from Ottoman territory (the Dodecanese until 1912 was a Turkish possession), I was deemed a national of a hostile country and my request was rejected by the US authorities.

But now things were different. Having been naturalized and officially an American for the last two years, and having studied, lived and worked in America for nearly two-and-a-half decades, there was no obstacle to my enlistment in the American army. Today, when I recollect how this story began, it seems a bit like a motion picture — many of which were filmed after the war. And, to be precise, are still being filmed.

It was summer. I was 42 years old in July 1942 when I angrily stopped two men who were walking behind me to ask them why they were following me. They did not deny it.

"Your audacity is limitless," I recall telling them. The two men smiled, as I remember, and asked me to accompany them to the FBI offices down the road from my business. They were federal agents and, indeed, they showed me identification to convince me. I would later learn they had been following me for six months without my noticing. Only lately did they become coarse and conspicuous in order to catch my attention, so that matters would move forward more easily. They wanted to know everything about me before trusting me, they said. I followed them to their offices. My adrenaline was peaking. I wondered what they might want from me. I would soon find out.

They were looking for Americans born in countries of occupied Europe and who, as speakers of the language of their countries of origin, could liaise with the Allied Command in Cairo for acts of sabotage against the Axis. I was later informed that they had recruited 13,500 citizens, both men and women — establishing a force roughly equal to a battalion — whose origins were from France, Italy, Romania and other countries under occupation with strategic significance for operational development. Of these, Greece had the greatest interest for the Allies, since through her territory passed shipments of raw materials, mainly chromium and bauxite. These Turkey supplied to Berlin, fueling the Nazi war machine, as the battles raged and the German warehouses ran short of munitions.

I listened to them, absorbing each word with all my senses. It took them a mere five minutes to get me excited and I was already confident they were not playing some sort of game with me. After an hour answering myriads of questions, I descended the stairs practically dancing. This was it! From this point onward, my life would change again. However, I had no idea to what extent my involvement in the war would turn matters on their head.

I was unmarried and my sole obligation at the time concerned the two employees at my business. I sold them my small lighting company for one dollar and presented myself for induction on January 3, 1943, at the Fort Meade compound, somewhere between Baltimore and Washington, D.C. The compound had been in operation since 1917 and had already been used for American military training during the First World War. Between 1942 and 1946, a total of 3.5 million Americans had trained there in all specializations, even army cooks.

After thirteen days I received transfer orders for Atlantic City, since my superiors decided I was to serve in the Army Air Corps. There, I received my basic training and accreditation in handling classified documents and instructions. Next came a transfer to the air corps base in Sioux Falls, South Dakota. Most of us who had been together in Atlantic City found ourselves together again there for training on radio usage, repair and assembly.

At Sioux Falls, I met for the first time a man who would mark my course: Philip Graham, a Harvard graduate from Washington, with whom I immediately bonded in a friendship that lasted to the end of the war. I knew little about him at first, for instance that he was married, although several years my junior. Philip liked to spend hours conversing, although I was slow to understand that, in essence, he sought to learn as much as he could about me beyond the bare facts that I was an electrical engineer and a Carnegie graduate.

Later, I also met his wife, a pleasant, modest, demure young American girl who often visited and stayed in a hotel in the city. The three of us passed many off-duty weekends together. It took quite a while for me to recognize that she — this modest woman who never, by word or deed, betrayed the origins of her heritage — was one of the most powerful women in America. Katharine, for that was her name, was the daughter of the owner of the *Washington Post* newspaper, the banker Eugene Meyer, who had saved the newspaper from bankruptcy in 1933. After the end of the war, Meyer handed the reins of the newspaper to his son-in-law, my friend Philip. For me, true to such an affinity, the sweet and humble Katharine was plainly and simply the wife of my friend.

The winter of 1942 was unusually severe and the dankness of South Dakota seemed to me more intense than even that of Pittsburgh. The chronic rhinitis from which I suffered after setting foot in America, being accustomed to the dry climate of Greece, had made a vexing reappearance. In order not to disturb others in the barracks, I survived literally stuck atop a radiator during the hours when others slept. Naturally enough, by staying awake for several nights, I soon lost the ability to focus on the intensive training lessons on the use of codes and wireless. And this did not escape the attention of my superiors.

And so, one night, my commanding officer approached me as I was returning to my bed.

"What's going on, Alex?" he asked.

I tried to scrape together shreds of an excuse, since my problem could no longer be concealed, and he ordered me to be on report the next morning. I was ordered to the infirmary for examinations. The doctors' diagnosis left no room for misconceptions: they judged my condition as very serious, to the point that they even suggested discharging me from the army. I was desperate. Such an outcome would totally negate all my dreams for finally being in my homeland and able to prove myself worthy of the confidence of the American government for the mission. I ran immediately to Philip to seek help. I still recall the calm with which he confronted me.

"Alex, you don't need to worry. Believe me, you are far too valuable to them to risk losing you."

This was not the only time Philip needed to console me. Moreover, he did not do so because of our friendship alone, but because he evidently knew something. Without doubt, I was the only one who still knew nothing about what lay in store.

When I once asked Philip whether he suggested that I should be entrusted with such a risky mission, he denied it. He continued to deny so even after the war and he did well. After all, what would be the point? All the same, I was confident that all those questions he asked me, during our long weekend conversations in Miami and later at his home in Washington during dinners with Katharine, were far from random. He wanted to get a sense of me. That is what he wanted: to evaluate my character well and to test my mettle. And, as it turned out, I passed the exams with flying colors.

*   *   *

"Alex, these are three class rotations. Choose to attend whichever suits you."

It was the disciplinarian voice of the captain. Puzzled, I took the paper in my hands and tried to meet his gaze, but he had already turned his back.

Somehow, November and all of December in 1942 passed with long hours and intensive medical monitoring and therapy. Around Christmas, having remained all along in the compound, I became hale and hearty.

At the beginning of January, we were all under restriction and there were neither leaves nor exit passes granted. We understood that something huge was in preparation. Within a few days, I received an order to collect my gear by separating my personal items from military equipment, which initially made me think they were preparing to discharge me from the army, despite Philip's assurances.

This was quickly disproved. As soon as I had collected my personal items, the duty officer handed me a sealed folder and a revolver. Destination: Washington — by train, of course.

"You will surrender the folder to the man who will meet you at the station as soon as you arrive," he told me.

"This will be the password," he added and then even more sternly said: "Understood? Give it to no one else. That's an order."

I was nearly dizzy as I boarded the train and even more in a spin when I arrived at my destination, since I had tried along the rather long route to sort out what all of this might mean. It helped that I had traveled alone in the train carriage — whether by coincidence or not, I never learned — and so there were no distractions.

When we pulled into the station, it was six o'clock in the afternoon. I emerged from the carriage with the certainty of meeting the man who would be waiting for me, but I saw no one coming towards me. Because the station was filled with soldiers, I began to pace to and fro in order to make my presence noticed — but to no avail.

After an hour, I began to worry. I waited another two hours before seeking the help of a military police officer. After listening to me, he led me to the office of the duty officer in charge of the military in the station. He asked me to state my orders, but I declined. I asked that they help me get to the closest Army Air Corps base in order to contact Sioux Falls. They drove me by jeep to Andrews Field. From there, I communicated with headquarters. The orders were clear. I was not to leave and to wait for the person who would come to meet me. I spent an entire night without closing my eyes for a second because of the tension.

At seven o'clock the next morning, my contact appeared. He gave the correct password and I handed him the folder. We then got into a State Department limousine and headed for Washington's famed Building Q.

I would later learn the name of the stranger I met for the first time that day; indeed, months later, we would work together from his post as Director of Intelligence, Greek Office, Middle East. He was Rodney Young, a youthful archaeologist who had studied classics at Princeton. He had lived in Greece for years before the war, had many archaeological excavations under his belt and spoke the language well. Indeed, he had such a deep love for the country that he voluntarily took part in the Greek-Italian conflict, during which he was seriously wounded.

The two of us were not able to discuss much during our first meeting. I did not ask why he failed to meet me at the station. I had already begun to enter into the spirit of the army people, especially this particular Service, which above all required confidentiality, a laconic disposition and strict adherence to instructions.

I was convinced that this entire affair, as it evolved, was another test in my evaluation, one that I had again passed with flying colors.

Young conveyed instructions pertaining to me. He said I would be given four days leave to return to my home in Pittsburgh before beginning a new training cycle lasting six or seven months in various camouflaged military camps around Washington. It turned out to be a very rigorous program with physical endurance exercises, parachute drops, rifle and revolver practice, explosives placement and disposal and, of course, wireless communications cryptographic code use.

Every Friday, we returned to Washington for a rest. One outcome that made me quite happy during my stay there was that I reunited with Philip, who had already been promoted to lieutenant colonel. We picked up where we left off and spent many weekends at their house in Washington. That was when I learned that Katharine was the daughter of Meyer of the *Washington Post*.

If something saddens me today, it is that I did not make an effort to see them again after the war and keep up our friendship. But with all that I went through, I did not want them to think that I would be doing so with ulterior motives — because I am certain that even one telephone call from them would have been enough to stop the persecution against me.

The Action Begins:
First Mission: Destination Cairo

Three difficult, round the clock and intense months went by until I received orders in early April to return to Pittsburgh and from there to try to communicate with my base, using the wireless. The very next day, a second urgent order arrived that ordered me to go back. To make sure there was no error, I asked for confirmation. The response I received was that it was an order which had to be executed immediately and without delay. I immediately took the first available plane and returned to base.

My mission was just beginning. In two days, I would depart for Cairo. My farewell with Philip and Katharine, who accompanied me to Andrews Field, was very moving. In Philip's eyes, I could see how much confidence he had in me, which influenced me profoundly and gave me great courage. Everything until this day, my enlistment, and the months of training now belonged to the past. All that was beginning today was no longer mere fantasy of the sort that I had relished in the evenings, as I lay stretched out on my bunk in the barracks at the base. It was a reality which I needed to be prepared to live in every respect.

'Am I ready?' I wondered, without giving myself an answer. There are not answers for everything.

My code name was "Gander." From this point onward, that would be my identity. I was not to reveal to anyone my true name, neither precisely who I was nor where I was from. I forgot this only once, in the beginning, and it cost me dearly. It was during my first travel by military aircraft, from Andrews Field with final destination Cairo, with six intermediate stopovers in Miami Brazil, Saint Helena, Accra, Cameroon and then Khartoum.

The airplane took off from the Army Air Corps base at Miami, filled with high-ranking American officers, some of Greek descent. Among them only one civilian passenger: Sophocles Venizelos. From his conversations with the others in Greek, I understood that he was en route to Cairo to take up an important position in Greece's government-in-exile. Indeed, as I later learned, he took over as Naval Secretary to the Tsouderos government in Cairo.

At least until the island of Saint Helena, my contacts with my fellow passengers had been clearly standard. I addressed everyone in

English, even those who spoke Greek among themselves, and all went well. No one concerned themselves with me, except when someone observed and indeed commented on the fact that I was given priority, while high-ranking officers with distinctive insignia waited in line with me. In the meantime, I was undisturbed in monitoring whatever they said. Most useful was the impression I formed of Venizelos, as my service in Cairo asked me about him later.

The damage was done when we stopped to refuel in Saint Helena, where we needed to stay for a couple of days for a small repair on the airplane. All of us stayed in the same lodgings, a simple hotel near the beach. On the following day, we went fishing for crabs. I got carried away and recognized by an American officer, named Kladakis, who hailed from the Dodecanese. We had known each other from the Dodecanese Youth of America. He did not conceal his surprise and, even though he had not remembered me at first, he seemed delighted to see me again and asked me where I was going. I may have told him I was merely a simple radio operator, but that I had revealed my identity drew a heavy reprimand.

It was obvious I had violated the most serious of all the rules we were taught during our training: not to reveal our identities. Of all the skills —leadership, self-confidence, creative thinking and speed in decision-making —, the rule I violated was regarded as the most important. For this reason, after we successfully passed all the training stages, the concluding phase in which everything was put to the test was the famous "relaxing" party. With free-flowing alcohol, music and conversation, most of us passed the most basic test without even being able to understand it had happened. Those who became carried away and revealed everything related to their mission and destination were automatically cut. Perhaps I was fortunate to have buckled on my way and, when the information arrived at headquarters, I had already been ordered to head towards Adrianople.

Cairo, a city for everyone

The first thing that struck me in Cairo was the city's hustle and bustle, the interminably small, dirty, sloping streets crossing it erratically, the crowds spread out all over the city and hundreds of markets of all sorts.

In its overflowing cafés, one could easily distinguish the locals from afar. Men dressed in djellabas and with narghiles in hand appeared, quite unlike foreigners in uniform and European attire. The latter, especially in the evenings, were accompanied to the most upscale haunts by their ladies, all very well-dressed and virtually shimmering. It was a genuine mosaic of people of every ethnic origin and class and, though all of them might have appeared relaxed, in reality no one was.

North Africa was considered a danger zone due to the German presence. Cairo and Casablanca, my last stop on my return to America two and a half years later, were the two cities known for bringing together spies of every origin. Most of them went about as businessmen and stayed in the most expensive hotels, also frequented by German officers. Others, in order to justify their presence in the countryside, professed to be geographers, meteorologists and even archaeologists. Still others, women mainly, purported to be spouses, though I doubt how many truly had this role.

Some, mainly British officers, preferred to rent spacious modern apartments in Jezerah (also called Zamalek), the small island that was also the most expensive district of the city overlooking the Nile and the golf course. Both the golf course and the polo field stood empty before sunset, since the heat was insufferable. They remained still and vacant between noon and six in the evening. Everyone remained shut indoors, under huge ceiling fans. It goes without saying that there were brothels for every willing wallet everywhere. The best known were on Claude Beis Street. In the vicinity of Ponte d'Angle was the fabled cabaret of Madame Bancia, perhaps the most foreigner-packed entertainment center in Cairo, where dancers swayed and shimmied to the rhythms of the celebrated belly dance. It was a time when many English marriages broke down. The soldiers who were there suddenly found themselves in the sunlight and the fresh air. Having left behind lands made soggy from constant rain, they were introduced to the joys of life, girls with bare arms and legs and, above all, willing.

The plethora of food, exotic fruits, drinks and cigarettes did not go unnoticed.

Life was literally delightful, but for everyone it almost hung by a thread. There was always the fear one's status would be revealed. You understood it when the door opened and suddenly loutish and gruff-voiced German officers entered and took over the best tables and, whilst being entertained, strafed everything around them with their gaze. In those moments, the atmosphere would become electrified. Everyone took up positions of readiness. You could smell it in the air despite the superficially calm manners and polite smiles. So, if the pianist stopped playing even for a fraction of a second and changed repertoire, you sensed pervasive nervousness spreading.

Much safer entertainment was had in the outdoor summer cinemas, of which there were several. I enjoyed staring into the night sky at the stars so high above. I had never been to an open-air cinema before and I was thrilled. A truly unique experience for an American who lived with cold and snow, ten months a year.

Black marketeers and local pickpockets were naturally not absent from the whole scene. The British, Irish, Scots, Greeks, Czechs, Cypriots, Poles, Maltese, South Africans, Rhodesians, Americans and Palestinians were easy targets. Most despised of all were the Italians, despite the pro-Italian sentiments of King Farouk. Meanwhile, and for reasons unknown, the Egyptians did not permit Australians to abide in Cairo and sent them to Palestine.

Of all the above, the British had secured the best places. Their command had occupied the entire Semiramis Hotel on the Nile. Their Middle East Office was in luxury apartments, a well-guarded bulwark behind wire mesh, in Garden City. Their practice in ferreting out networks of German spies was proverbial. They used prostitutes, card players and all sorts of criminals, even buying off imprisonment sentences.

When I arrived in Cairo, the chief of British Intelligence was Major Sansom. His reputation after a raid he made in the city, accompanied by Churchill's son-in-law Christopher Soma, was discussed for months. In that operation, he managed to penetrate Egyptian military circles — who also had little love for the Germans and the British — and captured a previously unknown young officer, who was none other than Anwar Sadat. It was actually said he was personally interrogated by Churchill himself, who happened to be there at the time.

Given this fascinating backdrop, I felt provincial and that was perfectly natural. If one excluded that I had rubbed shoulders with both prominent persons and non-city dwellers during my training in Washington, I was merely an American from a rather poor state, a Dodecannesean born in the poorest island of all, Karpathos.

In Cairo, the first person I met and reported to, at the OSS headquarters on Roustem Pasha Street, was Colonel Ulius L. Amoss. He told me they were awaiting the arrival of Rodney Young at any moment. Young would soon take over the Greek Desk of the OSS, under the General Administration Middle East and the orders of director Dr. Stephen B. L. Penrose, Jr., who had served as president of the American University of Beirut.

My first mission was to monitor the discussions of Greek officers and soldiers in the cafés. I was also asked to contact someone from the Resistance from Crete who was cooperating with the British and was in Cairo with his family.

I found him sitting alone in the coffee shop where we had agreed to meet. "Waiting for someone," he said, without clarifying anything further. I did not even ask if it could have been related to me and our own meeting. Ultimately, this "someone" never materialized. Perhaps he had seen me approach and opted not to appear.

Alex in Cairo before the commencement of his secret mission to Turkey.

I told him I was an American who spoke Greek because I had (supposedly) married a Greek woman. He observed straightaway that for an American I spoke the language quite well and introduced himself to me. He had a strong Cretan accent. He was called Petrakogiorgis and had the code name "Kapitanios Y." My issue was to persuade him to work with a couple of us, to which he had no objection. He was in fact willing to provide five hundred Cretan rebels for the needs of the Resistance. I bought a good deal of clothing and other items for him and his family, which were received with joy. What happened with the arrival of Young that changed everything, I would never learn. Even when I met him many years after the war, somewhere in the mid-1960s, he seemed unable to conceal the fact that our meeting had not at all been pleasant for him.

In the meantime, my collaboration with Young had begun. We were mapping out my mission in Greece for the collection of intelligence for the SI Branch, as it was known for short, when delayed information arrived about an irrevocable decision, namely that Greek Americans were not permitted to undertake operations in Greece. However, that directive, to my great satisfaction, was revised by the Director of the OSS, General Donovan.

The plan was for me to head to the Greek consulate at Adrianople, where a base for the British working with the Greek Resistance had been set up. I was furnished with a special passport issued by the government-in-exile of Prime Minster Tsouderos and presented myself to the Turkish authorities as an interpreter for the consulate. The formalities lasted for five or six weeks.

During my stay in Cairo, I came into contact with numerous government officials and Greek army officers who frequented the many cafés of the city. In that same period, I met a known Greek American who had been transferred to Cairo from a base in India. I happened to know his brothers who had a coffee shop of their own in Pittsburgh. He was a student in Greece and a member of EON, the National Youth Organization started by the Metaxas regime. He had emigrated to America upon an invitation of his brothers. When war broke out, he rushed to enlist in the US Army. His name was Dinos Katsafanas. We would often get caught up in arguments in a coffee shop about the political situation in Greece and the support of his family for the Metaxas regime. In Cairo, however, and under the conditions prevalent at the time, he found his métier: He dealt with extreme right-wing elements and would incriminate all and sundry for us — without exception, whether agreeable or not — drafting multi-page reports in antiquated Greek. His reports were useful to us because they contained much information on the political and military situation in Greece.

This is Georgiades' passport issued by the Greek diplomatic mission to Cairo on behalf of the exiled government. His accreditation is declared to the Turkish authorities as an interpreter at the Greek General Consulate in Adrianople (or Edirne).

To the uninitiated, I presented myself merely as a Greek businessman from Khartoum who had come to Cairo for medical treatment and was interested in learning news from Greece so that, upon my return to Sudan, I could inform other Greeks living there. It was then that I met Colonels

Hadzistavris and Kladakis, cousin of the milkman from New York and a co-traveler of mine on the trip from America to Cairo. Kladakis, specifically, was professor of architecture at the Metsovion Polytechnic in Athens. Both Hadzistavris and Kladakis had been cashiered, due to British intervention, as responsible for the rebellion in the Gaza camp and since then had been labeled the "Red Colonels." Their companion of the same ideological proclivity was Roussos, whom I would meet much later in Evros.

Subsequently, these three would take divergent paths. The first sought refuge in the Congo. Kladakis remained in Egypt and for years I did not know what became of him. When I met him again in 1965, he told me that while there he worked for the Political Committee of National Liberation, the **PEEA**, commonly known as the "Mountain Government." This was a type of government within occupied Greece that planned secret elections and was preparing to overthrow the Tsouderos government-in-exile and to form a national unity government. The proposal immediately found supporters within Cairo's military circles, but also encountered a strident reaction on the part of the British and Tsouderos himself.

Arrival in Adrianople

It was already summer when I arrived in Adrianople, following a stopover in Istanbul to meet with Captain Jerome Sperling, then head of our base and handler of our correspondence via diplomatic pouch. Sperling, whose pseudonym was "Sparrow," was an archaeologist with extensive experience in the digs in Troy. As our liaison with the secret intelligence service of Turkey, the infamous *Emniyet* (literally, "Security"; truncated from of *Milli Emniyet Hizmeti*, or National Security Service), Sperling brought me into contact with Gelal Bey, with whom in subsequent months I developed friendly relations. Gelal Bey was the director of Turkey's security authorities, which would undertake to protect me on Turkish soil.

In Istanbul, I also met with Kampalouris, general consul in Adrianople. On July 14, I finally arrived at my destination. The first thing that impressed me was the number of people going to the consulate. I could not understand how many were regular employees, how many were locals and how many were Greeks from occupied Greece. Some were even British. They spent hours holed up in the consul's office conferring with him. There was an overall atmosphere of secrecy. I observed that, whenever I passed by, they fell silent and all treated me as a foreign intruder.

It is true that I tried chatting with some, initially for quite ordinary matters such as a "good day" greeting, to get the lay of the land and for personal needs of daily life.

From the conversations, I realized the triple occupation of the country barely had any impact on the perdurable Hellenic soul and, thus, the long-familiar wrangling about political affairs continued unabated. There were those who maintained that Greece would never be truly free and instead would forever be under the tutelage of one or the other strong foreign power, regardless of which power that might be. Most banked on the British, others on the French and the Russians and last of all came the Americans. There, I met Roussos for the first time, a Greek-Egyptian member of the Cairo government. Roussos, in fact, urged me to pay attention to what I heard inside the consulate.

"Are you listening to them?" he asked me one day. "Pay close attention to them. If you take note of their words, you will learn a lot."

The same was echoed by General Bakirtzis, who was responsible for ELAS of Thrace and for the PEEA.

All I knew was that I had to work with British Intelligence to collect information from occupied Greece and Bulgaria. Since I had minimal briefings from my own side before departure concerning the conditions that awaited me, I decided to travel to Ankara to meet Greek Ambassador Rafael Raphael. I found him equally restrained, if not to say, even colder, as if signaling that he was wasting his time by speaking with me. He used evasive speech and even that seemed forced. In my discussions with Young, later, I learned that neither of the two diplomats — the consul and the ambassador — appreciated my presence there. The reason was nothing more than British annoyance over the fact that an American service would entangle them. Indeed, Raphael had written extensive reports to Prime Minister Tsouderos himself in Cairo, asking for my removal, saying that I was provoking a backlash from "our British friends." To calm these reactions, he requested me to leave. Furthermore, for whatever period I stayed, I was ordered to keep the consul briefed on everything: my activities and, in particular, my contacts and my every movement within Turkey.

Alex with two of his agents

It was then that I began to realize that something was not quite right, and I would soon need to deal with much more serious problems. At the outset, the initial thing I was asked to do was restore the flow of intelligence from occupied Evros, since, according to Raphael, a British Intelligence network had been discovered and destroyed by the Germans. Thirty-six agents had been executed. Another sixty-nine had been warned and escaped to Cairo via Turkey. Among them was a reserve officer of the Greek Army, a colonel and mayor of Soufli, Panayiotis Demertzis, who fled by crossing the Evros with two or three others still in the consulate at Adrianople. Apparently, it was they whom I saw going in and out at the consulate.

In order to lead the Turks astray, British Intelligence had been installed in a rented building near the Greek Consulate. In essence, however, their interests were inextricably intertwined. It was obvious that any information given to the Consul — since Raphael had demanded this from Ankara — would arrive automatically to British eyes and ears, with whatever that might entail. I had to alert my superiors in Cairo immediately.

"But how?" I wondered.

I had instinctively sniffed out the danger early on. My base in the consulate had not yet been established nor had I begun to use the wireless. The icing on the cake and what convinced me that the climate was totally hostile toward me were the minced words from the military attaché of the Greek Embassy in Ankara who advised me that it would be better for me to return to Cairo.

That was it. Urgently needing to meet my chief of station, I made a beeline for Istanbul. I found Jerry (Sperling) in his office. Kampalouris was with him. They must have been engaged in discussion for quite a while. Both seemed truly troubled, almost devastated. In the meeting, the latter kept up the appearances of his diplomatic capacity. He showed no annoyance by my entrance, which was surely unanticipated, or by Sperling's forthrightness when he requested that every assistance be made available.

"Mr. Consul, the presence of Mr. Georgiades here is of vital importance for us," he said.

I do not know whether Sperling analyzed well the psychological implications, but I noticed he swallowed hard while nodding his head in agreement.

Georgiades repairing his radio in his office at the Greek Consulate in Edirne.

After my credentials were first formally announced, with the aid of my chief of station, to the Turkish authorities, I returned to Adrianople —— to establish my base under the code name "Pittsburgh." I began using the wireless, initially on a merely circumstantial basis. I continued to believe that the information I sent went beforehand to British Intelligence and afterwards to my compatriots.

My fears were confirmed when I commenced work with Demertzis, who, it should be said, proved to be highly cooperative. Demertzis worked from a British Intelligence building near the border. His job was to meet refugees who had been chased out of Evros and to acquire intelligence about Greece from them. A good deal of information came from Turkish border guards who used to frequent the railway station of the "Long Bridge," as we called it (*Uzun Köprü* in Turkish), in Evros, just across from Pythian Bridge connecting Greece with Turkey. Of course, little of that information was worthwhile because, to my great disappointment, the majority did not deal with the enemy but EAM and its commanders, intending to undermine them. It was the same frustration I felt when, by chance, some British Intelligence cables fell into my hands. Few of them concerned German movements and fewer still made mention of penetration actions in neighboring Bulgaria, which was then a planning priority of the Allies.

One day, while I was talking with the vice-consul, Venetziano, and Liza Dimitriadou, a young lady who worked as a secretary — two of the consulate staff that included a well-regarded older woman, Melpomeni, who was the consul's cook — and a young man who worked as an attendant, the former consulate cook, named Giorgos Tsiaparas, entered the consulate. He had just been released from prison. Because he spoke Turkish very well, he was used for errands, mainly shopping. Since he had many acquaintances among Turkish merchants, he became involved at one point with the black-market gold and currency exchanges and, as a result, was arrested. He had been in prison for several months and now, upon being released, had come by to say his goodbyes before leaving for Cairo.

Liza Dimitriadou, secretary of the Greek Consul in Edirne.

From the first instance, I understood that he was strikingly smart, shrewd and slippery. Seeing that the Turks assigned me an Armenian interpreter who perpetually abandoned me and left the city for family reasons, as he claimed, I asked Tsiaparas to stay on as my aide. Naturally, the Turks did not care for this at all, but I was enthusiastic to finally have someone astute and alert to work with. I could now put into practice the plan I had been preparing for days, aware that, if matters were left on this path, we would hit a dead end.

Inasmuch as orders from Cairo were sluggish in arriving, I was on edge due to a series of events, such as the Italian capitulation which had emboldened the Germans. At the same time, a strange inertia held sway at the consulate and so I took the initiative to act by preparing my passage to Greece. Instructions could not possibly be delayed further, I thought.

I was reluctant to talk about these matters with Tsiaparas inside the consulate, so I took him outside. While we walked through the city, he confided to me the information, literally whispering in my ear, that there was a suitable person to put me in contact with the guerrillas and guide me, with comparative safety, through Evros to their lairs. Unfortunately, this person had been severely wounded by Turkish border guards in some dungeon in the detention facilities of the Adrianople Police Station.

This was not uncommon. Large numbers of Greeks, including women and small children, who attempted to cross the Evros to safety fell victim to the border guards. Others swam and were swept away by currents and drowned. And others still, despite having paid the ill-famed baksheesh to the Turks in advance, would set foot on the riverbank across only to be robbed of all their possessions. The majority were stripped naked and had their clothes stolen. Then, they were killed.

The son of the Mayor of a Turkish border village (Saranlı) used to cross the Evros River.

The man in question was one of the couriers of Panayiotis Demertzis, who conveyed messages to the consulate. Tsiaparas knew him. The information about his injuries was the result of eavesdropping on the conversations of Turks in a city café. He told me the man's name: Giorgos Valasidis. Although he knew the goings-on of the consulate, Tsiaparas said, they had done nothing to save that hapless man and abandoned him in the grip of the Turkish Security Authorities.

I thought hard before deciding what to do. In the end, I concluded that I must speak to my Turkish liaison officer, Gelal Bey. He figured things out and learned where the man was being held and allowed me to visit him. I found him in a truly bad state. He had a deep head wound which had not healed properly and stank. With Gelal's help, he was transferred to hospital and saved, literally, at the last minute. I later learned that, at some point, due to this severe injury, he lost his sight entirely.

Days passed. I waited for Valasidis to get well in order to re-enter Evros and notify the guerrillas that I wanted to contact them. In the meantime, Cairo's much-awaited instructions arrived. They agreed for me to cooperate with the Greek guerrillas, but in no case did they wish me to risk injury by entering Greek territory. This would be done by others: the couriers I would find and trust. This was no easy task, nor could it be accomplished overnight. Meanwhile, time was pressing. I briefed Gelal Bey, claiming that I had received orders to enter Greece, so at least as not to be at risk from the Turks and in preparation for the big operation.

A week later, Valasidis returned with good news. He brought with him two guerrillas: Panos Farfaras and Thodoros Mitas or "Moravas." Panos and his brother Vasilis had escaped from the Didymoteichon prisons, after their brother Elias, caught in a Germans ambush at Pyrgos Orestiada, was horribly tortured and executed. They had gone to the mountains with Moravas, who was also from Orestiada. Farfaras and Moravas were veterans of the Greek-Albanian conflict and declared themselves to be communists, no matter that they had but scant knowledge of communist theory.

I used these two as my couriers throughout the time I stayed up there, nearly thirteen months.

"He was tall, wiry, and wore oval-frame glasses that hid two
uneasy eyes; he weighed his words, was direct and candid."
These exact words were used to describe Georgiades by
one of the ELAS guerrillas who came to know him at the
Evros region. He added: "Those who sent him to us made
an excellent choice, because he would not flinch before
clear and present dangers, and no one could stop him from
doing what he was set on doing."

During the same period, which would have been early September,
I made another big decision: to abandon the security of the consulate.
Kampalouris had learned of my contacts from Demertzis, whom he did
not like at all, and he pressed me to give him reports on my movements.
I asked approval from my chief of station in Istanbul, writing, on August
13, that the situation reminded me of a sieve because everyone knows
everything. Accommodation to establish my base outside the consulate
was found with Gelal's help. In fact, the authorities had even designated a
guard to patrol the area around the dwelling, despite pressure on Turkey

from the German embassy there to cease providing a security umbrella and facilitating actions of the Allies in its territory.

It was then that the Turkish government issued a decree halting all activities in Adrianople. In view of the circumstances, I met Gelal Bey with the aid of Sperling in Istanbul and told him that I would not be returning to Adrianople, despite the implications for US-Turkish relations. Gelal decided to take matters into his own hands. He asked me to return to base and stay silent for two weeks without arousing suspicions. In the meantime, he would change all the security personnel in the vicinity, so that the new liaisons would have no idea about the prohibition that was still in force.

I developed with Gelal Bey a relationship that was familiar and friendly. He had greatly appreciated that, during a fundraiser for the Turkish Red Crescent, I had given him two thousand Turkish lira (about one thousand dollars). He was extremely grateful for that. It was a pity that not long afterward he was replaced by another officer, Sahin Targin, though I did not get on poorly with him, either.

But Gelal — who, in the meantime, had been promoted to head *Emniyet* — took care to inform me before leaving that I should not trust Tsiaparas and perhaps he was not wrong. Not because he was a traitor, but because his adventure made him susceptible to breaking under pressure if caught again. I spoke to Sperling, who promptly rushed to find a solution. It was obvious that the ease with which he appeared to find expeditious solutions was due to instructions arriving from Cairo and that the plan I was preparing was significant.

Sperling recommended to me his own highly competent and cooperative translator, a graduate of the British Naval School, Giorgos Mavris, whose brother, Manolis, was willing to work with me. Manolis had studied in England and in Greece, but with the war he turned to Istanbul and finished law school there. He spoke three languages with ease, including Turkish. These days, I learned that he practises law in Athens. We communicate quite regularly. Our cooperation was excellent and he was literally my right hand while I was in Adrianople. For his ability and dedication, as well as the trust shown, I mentioned him in several of my references at the time. Perhaps that was the reason why, as I learned after the war, Donovan, who traveled to Greece to attend the famous Polk trial, requested that the embassy use him as its official translator.

Alexander Georgiades second from the left at Arnavutköy, a suburb of Istanbul.
Next to him the father and his assistant in OSS George Mavris.

My acquaintance with these two brothers, however, held in reserve another surprise that I would never have expected, particularly not in that specific period of my life, when I lived in a state of high tension. It shook me emotionally. One Sunday, they invited me to dine with their parents at Arnavutköy, a suburb of Istanbul. I learned that both had origins from Kassos and, indeed, the mother had my father as a teacher. Imagine how small the world seemed to me.

This invitation coincided with my decision to leave the consulate. Specifically, upon returning on the evening of that same Sunday, I learned that Kampalouris was asking for me urgently. I wondered what he might want. It tormented me until I arrived at his office.

He was as terse as ever, but also aggressive. He appeared furious and was waiting upright with a low-light lamp lit on his desk. He must have been there for a long time and looked like a lion in its cage. He wanted to announce that, due to my lack of willingness to cooperate with him, he would send a cable to skewer me with the Greek government in Cairo. And, naturally, he did so. In such things he was quite consistent.

Sophocles Venizelos was minister of foreign affairs at that time and had told Kampalouris that, during our multi-day trip from America to Cairo, the reason I was slow to reveal that I knew Greek was because I monitored what he said, so as to report on his character to the American government. So, he held a grudge. And his slander and denigration continued. Naturally, without result.

Raphael also tried to do the same from Ankara by writing to Papandreou, who succeeded Tsouderos as prime minster. Indeed, he wrote the worst about me: that I was a cad and an aggrandized snob who would not tell them what work I did. Hyper-sensitive things, that is.

The world was being lost, dozens were dying every day in battles and from starvation in the cities and here they were seated in their offices, with their drivers, their beautiful homes, close to their families, far from danger, carrying on with their daily routines. Their minds were full of grandeur and protocols. But Papandreou left him dumbstruck when he answered that my job was precisely that: not to tell anyone what I did. Those who needed to know knew and that was sufficient.

The Passage to Evros

As the situation deteriorated constantly inside and outside the consulate, dozens of refugees waited to cross the border. They sought deliverance on Turkish soil, due to the terrorism unleashed in Evros by the rebel leader Odysseus. Since Turkey was hindering their entry, I understood that every hour I delayed contact with the guerrillas was fatal and destructive for my mission. After being informed by British Intelligence and the Greek government-in-exile of the chaos that prevailed here, headquarters in Cairo refused to approve my entry into Evros, assessing that my life would be at risk. The instructions I received were to try to come into contact with ELAS and begin consultations with them, but only via couriers.

Indeed, on September 29, 1943, I sent Tsiaparas to Evros to meet their leadership and ask them to travel somewhere near the border in order that we could talk. He was gone for three days. When he returned, he had three other companions with him. They stayed in Adrianople for two days and we tried to work out what to do. I explained that my mission was to collect intelligence on the movements of the Germans and that I had neither orders nor intent to interfere with their political differences. They were plainspoken and made it clear that, while I had not convinced them that I had no connections or contacts with the government or the British, they were all the same obliged to convey my message to their leader, Odysseus.

After twelve days, they returned with a letter from their leader which said I was only welcome if I were willing to cooperate honestly with them, otherwise my life and the lives of my associates would be in jeopardy. The letter also mentioned that in Laina, a village 85 km south of Adrianople, armed guards would meet me to lead me to their hideaway. The date for the meeting was set on October 25. I immediately alerted Sahin to ensure my safe passage there from the Turkish side. Sahin was even willing to locate a house somewhere nearby for my meetings that would allow me to have easy communication from Bulgarian-occupied territories to the Mediterranean. On the evening of that day, I was already crossing the river.

Dawn found us on the opposite bank. The first thing I remember was how everything around me was redolent, even ambrosial. The earth exuded the fresh dew of the morning mist. Shrubs, dried cobs and trees seemed different to me here, more beautiful. I stayed silent for a few minutes to look across to where my gaze was lost on the horizon of the Thracian land. And that land, like an open maternal embrace, was welcoming before me. I bent over and kissed the soil of my homeland upon which I now strode again after twenty-five years.

And then something happened that I will never forget as long as I live. My two hard-nosed escorts, Farfaras and Moravas, who would lead me to the guerrillas' hideaway, stood and stared at me with tear-filled eyes. It is a scene that will always be etched within me. No one can take it away. After all that happened afterwards, no one can ever tell me that these fighters were traitors and did not love their homeland as much as I.

Thodoros Mitas or Moravas, one of his two Greek guerrilla guides
who helped Alex to cross the Evros River.

The sun had now risen higher and we were still walking. We had left the plain behind and climbed the mountain that rose on our left. All along our route, we encountered guards to monitor our safe passage. At some point, we reached a hill encircled by huge rocks with lookouts on guard. It was the Gybrena hideaway. We had arrived without peril. It was, however, a matter of chance, since German public patrols were frequent and we needed to cross it twice. We stopped somewhere to drink a little water from our flasks.

Alex upon his first arrival to Greece together with Greek guerrillas
just received ammunition from Cairo.

Alex at the hideout of the Greek guerrillas in Lefkimi.

Our journey lasted five hours. We found them at mealtime. As I figured, there must have been about eighty to one hundred of them. Most were unshaven and bearded, but all were tatterdemalions. Among them were some women rebels and one of them, indeed, was a teacher. Among their leadership, there were two more teachers, one doctor, two lawyers and a bank clerk.

"Welcome, American!" It was the voice of their leader, who welcomed me.

"Welcome, welcome!" Others rose to repeat the greeting. They surrounded me, looking me over, up and down, filled with curiosity.

They invited me to eat with them: grilled goat and wine. Farfaras and Moravas had already spread themselves out on the ground and had begun to eat, hungry from the night before.

I sat near Odysseus, as they called their leader, who had succeeded Aris after his execution by the Germans. Aris, who was from Lagadas, had been captured after being entrapped by the Bulgarians in Komotini the previous February and they in turn had handed him over to the Germans for interrogation. He was the one who knew everyone and everything, even the names of the dogs of the Evros shepherds, so they told me, but his lips remained sealed. He pretended to show them the guerrillas' hideaways and with handcuff-bound hands came out with them on the mountain. There, somewhere near a place called Vouva, he tried to flee and the Germans strafed him.

Two months went by after the death of Aris without leadership. Until a man who was unknown to them appeared out of nowhere, accompanied by a woman from Soufli.

He said he was called Odysseus and that the party had sent him, but he had no papers with him to prove it was so. Contrariwise, while trying to win the confidence of the locals, he seemed to cultivate the impression that he was none other than Mitsos Partsalides, a leading member of the KKE (Greek Communist Party). One month later, while I was in Dadia, a large village in Evros, a magazine caught my attention with a photo of the real Partsalides, a leading member of the KKE and mayor of Kavala. I showed it to Tiacas — a lawyer, intellectual and party member under the pseudonym "Lycurgus" — and we then notified Kritonas and Moravas. They said that they needed to contact the Thessaloniki headquarters immediately. As there was no other way, they sent Tiacas' wife, with the alibi that she needed a doctor, in order to alert the leadership and then return with orders. The mere thought that Odysseus might be an agent of the notorious Bulgarian Ohrana, who collaborated with the Germans, made us feel as if the ground fell away from beneath our feet.

In the meanwhile, from the first moment I met him, I noticed all his facial details as he spoke. As a person, I did not care for him in the slightest. Not only because he was exceedingly grotesque, but because there was something about the manner in which he expressed himself, the movements of his hands and the pompous words he resorted to when speaking of resistance.

After two or three bites, I stopped eating to respond to their questions, which came like rapid fire.

They wanted to learn everything about me: where I was from; whether I had a family and children; what orders I had; how long I intended to stay there with them. They were furious with the British, who through their tactics of sending weapons to the fascists, to German collaborators and the Bulgarians, who, instead of fighting the enemy, had turned their guns against them.

"As we speak, you'll not see a single one of them here," he told me. "They have withdrawn to the consulate, but from there they continue their treacherous work. The agents of Tsaus Anton have also passed into Bulgaria for security. There, they collaborate with Bulgarian fascists and await a suitable time to strike us here. But we don't cower. The only thing we need is weapons. Will your people give them to us or will they sell us out as the filthy British did?"

Listening to their leader, everyone nodded their heads to signal they endorsed what he said.

I took the floor immediately. I asked how many they were and if there were other armed men.

They told me there were others scattered about in smaller hideaways and that they could form up to three thousand men, as long as they found weapons.

I made clear at the outset that I could not provide them with arms, but I could convey their needs to my Service in Cairo. The aid I could offer was only in foodstuffs, medicine, for which there was a dire need because of malaria, paper, ink, hectograph duplicators, radios and batteries. I gave them a few wristwatches I had taken along with me and money. In exchange for our cooperation, I asked them to regularly give me intelligence on the strength and movements of Germans in the region as well as information from inside Bulgaria.

They may not have been enthusiastic because they had different expectations from me, but they accepted to cooperate in the hope that, when I returned, I would bring better news and, above all, weapons.

"Arms, Alekos! We want arms! Otherwise, the enemies will never budge from here!"

Thus came a voice from one to my right and all who heard him instantly applauded. They had already begun calling me Alekos, my name in Greek, which seemed a positive sign and a clear example of friendship and trust.

I stayed with them for three days the first time. Their daily program was more or less identical unless there was a sudden incident or an organized attack. There were many conversations, plans were exhaustively discussed, couriers came from Bulgaria or Adrianople. The closest was Nea Vyssa where the British and British Intelligence had set up a pseudo-base. Many of their debates concerned their suspicions of traitors and persons bought off by the British, who were trying to split their forces and gain information about their plans and impending moves. Many people became victims of that sick climate and were executed. However, the major purges were made under Odysseus' leadership, when a climate of terror spread to Evros that threatened to blow the resistance movement into the air.

One of the first things to impress me was their organization. These were, in the main, illiterate, ordinary laborers and stockbreeders with scant military experience but with tremendous discipline and an emergency system when needed. One night as we slept, everyone was suddenly awakened, stood upright and took up arms as they heard bells ringing in a neighboring village. They left me behind with only a couple of guards and were on their way immediately. I asked what had happened and was told that looting had developed into a scourge. Some pony-tailed Greeks stole the animals from within the pens and led them up to the Turkish border through Evros. There, they sold them to Turks at the border. When this was noticed, if it was in the first place, the village notified the rebels, who caught the looters and returned the animals to their owners.

So, it was that evening. And the villagers were so overjoyed that they came out of their homes in the night, surrounded the rebels in the village square and embraced them. Later, I heard from locals that the self-administration and security system that the guerrillas had established had nothing to do with the guarding of villages before the war. They had shown themselves to be exceptional.

Together with Panos and Moravas, I returned to Adrianople. Loads of work awaited me. I had to make urgent contact with Cairo, to convey the news to my superiors. And of course, I needed to gather what was promised to the rebels. The US army did not know quinine, so they used another drug, but I thought they would be suspicious. Fortunately, the Turkish army had recently acquired a large supply of quinine, so I was able to buy enough to cover the needs of the year.

Meanwhile, news spread like wildfire inside the consulate that during my absence I was in Evros. One could understand it from their faces and double-talk. I tried to ignore it and only spoke to them once, when I asked for help from the wireless operator used by British Intelligence who had now been transferred to Nea Vyssa. His name was Nikos Katzouros. The request was granted with enthusiasm and I was not slow in understanding why. They thought Katzouros would have access to the information I sent to Cairo. But they did not count on me executing the encryption and decryption on my own. Their joyfulness was misplaced.

Nick Katzouros, the radioman of the Greek consulate at Edirne
with the secretary of the consul, Liza Dimitriadou.

Another great facilitation, thanks to Gelal, was that I was able to acquire an automobile, which I bought in Istanbul and was driven by Targin. The purchase was approved by Sperling because the train on the Istanbul-Thessaloniki route stopped at a suburb of Adrianople about thirty-five miles south of the city, which made travel extremely difficult for me.

Meanwhile, to the great satisfaction of my Service, my contacts with the guerrillas became more frequent. The Service was preparing a key Special Operations Branch action plan under Major Kellis for sabotage operations against infrastructure targets of the occupiers. However, things were otherwise at the consulate and Raphael in Ankara, who was really beside himself. What they wrote to the government in Cairo is indescribable. They had already abandoned the effort to go against me personally, seeing that it did not work. So, they had begun a series of analyses to assess politically the new reality that my action there was shaping: supposedly a great deal of confusion and anxiety prevailed in the local community, since what they understood is that the Greek government, through this Service and its activities — meaning me — is in effect siding with "murderers and other criminal elements" with known communists, after having neutralized an Allied Service — meaning, of course, British Intelligence. Concerning the action of the Major Miller, the ambassador's documents were, of course, silent. This British major had arrived in the region one month after me, in August 1943, who scoured Eastern Macedonia, sowing terror among the Greek population, with the ranks of Tsaus Anton and every sort of pillager.

What a case that Tsaus Anton was. I think serpents like him are rarely born. Hiding behind his pseudonym was a certain Antonis Fosteridis, born in Pontus, who before the war was a rural constable at Krinides Kavalas. This degenerate was accused by the Bulgarians for the murder of his wife, who had been an obstacle to his extramarital relationships, and was imprisoned, but escaped and went into hiding at Paggaio. There, he organized a predatory gang that ravaged the villages, killing men and defrauding women, until at some point the vehemently anti-communist Tsaus Anton came into contact with the notorious Miller. This is how their collaboration began. For years, the inhabitants remembered and spoke with revulsion of the incident when, as they raped the wife of a rebel in the Bulgarian-occupied zone, she knew that after a Bulgarian ambush they would execute her husband.

Those who knew him say he would even dress up as a vagabond
riding a donkey in order to escape attention.

The Insidious Role of the British and of British Intelligence

With every passing day, I understood that the aberrant and unseemly struggle between the Allies was intense and certainly began from above. Later, I learned that it was Roosevelt's idea to ask Churchill to withdraw British Intelligence from the Evros region and insert Americans into the area. The reasons were dual. On the one hand, Evros was a strategically important zone through which railway wagons passed with bauxite and other raw materials from Turkey to feed the Axis war machine in Berlin. On the other hand, the British were playing political games and cared more for the country's post-war situation and the return of the monarchy. That is why they put weapons in the hands of the most extreme and lumpen elements against EAM, which was the only one calling upon the people to engage in resistance, and ELAS, which was its military arm and the only one that fought the occupiers. Here, ELAS did not have one but two armies to deal with: the Bulgarians and the Germans together. The latter, after the Macedonian and Thracian surrender to Bulgaria in exchange for freeing the pathway to attack Greece, had kept under their control the sensitive zone along the Greek-Turkish border and a few miles into the hinterland. From there, they could pass much-needed raw materials to maintain the Axis war machine.

But then, by their flagrant and cowardly policies, all the British had achieved was to sow discord and division among the people. The result was that one half regarded the other half as agents and traitors and slit each other's throats, leaving the subjugators undisturbed.

Such news, of course, soon reached the Allied Headquarters in Cairo and from there Washington, where it was deemed appropriate for the British to be replaced by the Americans and for the OSS to take action.

If it is true that centuries ago an ancient Greek tragic poet said that the one thing that is definitely lost in a war is the truth, I am quite afraid that it will take several decades to uncover the dishonorable role the British then played at the expense of the Greek people.

Their hypocrisy had no limits. Unfortunately, things did not calm down even after Roosevelt's telephone call to Churchill and the withdrawal of British Intelligence from Evros.

The British agents initially holed themselves up in the Greek consulate, in full knowledge of the Turks, and engaged in the same tactics as before. With the help of Demertzis, they caught those crossing into Evros in order to extract information and then, accordingly, supplied weapons first to the EAM and then to the monarcho-fascists. The former to strike the enemy, the latter to rout out the former.

The director of movements was MI6 agent Harold Gibson, established in Istanbul, supervised by Kampalouris and responsible for contacts with Demertzis' liaisons. They gave orders to the notorious Major Miller, who was responsible for the Thrace office operating in Evros.

After the experience they had from their meeting with Sperling's new chief, a banker from Chicago named Macfarland, who took over the OSS office in Istanbul in the spring of 1943 and who was ignorant of European affairs, they believed that we were obtuse and credulous. They called us *Amerikanakia* or "little Americans," as they did all over Greece and did with us as they pleased. Only in my case, their ideas were way off beam and on the wrong end of the stick. Because I was not only American, but Greek as well. Their tricks did not work on me. That was not the only reason that made me appreciate how accurate General Donovan had been in canceling the ban on action by American agents in their countries of origin. I am confident that it would have been equally advantageous for the allied camp to include OSS agents born in France, Italy and other European countries under occupation. And of course it was not simply language skills that made them useful. It was the mentality, the culture and the differences in perceptions and interpretations of situations that an American who had not lived in Europe would find difficult to comprehend.

Naturally, regarding Anglo-American antagonism, which emerged right in the middle of the war and even more vehemently between their secret services, the scales were clearly tipped in favor of the British, who had already had a tradition in this field since the Crimean War and the Greek Revolution.

America was then taking its first steps, having taken lessons from the First World War just a few decades prior.

The Gibsons, for instance, were born agents. British brothers born in Russia, Archibald and Harold were both agents of MI6 before the war:

the former as a London *Times* correspondent in Bucharest and the latter in Prague before being sent to Istanbul. And as if this were not enough, both had married daughters of the La Fontaine and Whittall families, British families that were permanently established in Istanbul and were likewise MI6. Indeed, one member of the Whittall family, also accredited to their embassy, was the liaison with the "friendly foreign service," a euphemism meaning the Zionists. In other words, we are talking about jackals.

Terror Erupts in Evros at the Most Critical Moment

While my cooperation with Odysseus and EAM was proceeding in good order and the information I was communicating to Cairo was enough to convince my Office that conditions were favorable for sending a group from the Special Operations branch to proceed with sabotage, I was asked what calamity, in my opinion, would cause the most damage. I did not need to think about it much. It was, of course, the bridge at Pythion, where railways linked Turkey to Greece and Central Europe. Whatever other smaller bridge of secondary importance might be destroyed, I wrote to them, would be quickly rebuilt by the Germans and the populace would again pay in reprisals. Of course, such a crude course of action could displease the Turks and so, in my view, the absolutely perfect time had to be chosen.

For some days, I had no news from Cairo, until word reached me that a SO team led by Captain James Kellis had arrived in Istanbul. Kellis arrived first. Sperling met him at the Haydarpaşa Gar railway terminal, taking all necessary precautions. He was dressed in a white trench coat, he offered his right hand in greeting and, as soon as he saw the ruby ring, he understood. Following him in a black sedan automobile, he set off for the OSS offices. Two days later, two other Greek-American wireless operators arrived: Spyros Kaponis, who was known as Gus, and Mike Angelos. The three of them were expecting two more individuals, who would arrive from the Çeşme base. These were a naval officer named Everett Athens and a marine whom I had already met since he had been my demolitions trainer. The latter would be the detonator.

My job was to take them into Greece with the help of ELAS. I went to Istanbul to meet them. Kellis struck me as very smart and capable, what we call a stalwart. We made our recommendations and stayed together a few days, I then took to the road and returned to Adrianople. I needed to set in motion the plan for the team to transit into Greek territory.

In Adrianople, bad news caught me completely unprepared. Targin came to find me to tell me that dozens of refugees had spent the last few days in Turkey because of the climate of terror which had spread in Evros following Odysseus's orders to execute all those who, until then, had been in touch with the Greek consulate and the British.

I raced to Uzun Köprü to meet with the refugees in order to crosscheck the information.

Gus Kaponis, the wireless operator of SO Chicago Mission that blew
the two bridges in Alexandroupolis and Svilengrand.

They told me the same things. I learned there that the rallying cry that came forth from the organizations was "fire and axe to the Anglophiles." The reason for this was the discovery of a network that supplied arms to traitors among the rebel groups. These weapons had been sent by the British with the help of Musa Kâzim Karabekir at Ipsala. From there, Miller distributed them to opponents of EAM, some of whom had even succeeded in deceiving Odysseus himself and had gone up into the mountains with his guerrillas. Karabekir's role was especially loathsome. He despised the Greeks from the era of the Asia Minor Catastrophe when, as a general of Kemal, he had under his command the most fanatic marauder bands, the *çetes*, who had massacred us. He continued, despite his advanced age, to want to harm Greece. Unfortunately, his property, an expansive and fertile tract, was very close to the border. The reason for which could not have been unrelated to Kemal's decision to grant him this estate as a reward for his services and his dedication. From there, the aging general could control all movements and facilitate all illegal activities.

Alex in civilian clothes with his local assistants
Mitso and Valasidis in Edirne.

Unfortunately, much blood was spilled during the winter of 1943, particularly during the days when I was in Istanbul. People who could have fought the enemy were unjustly lost and consciences devastated within an incredible climate of suspicion and terrorism that spread like cancer, reaching even ordinary people, even widows with small children. As expected, of course, this worked against EAM. Later, I learned that orders were given by someone to eliminate me, but I was pardoned because I was still valuable. Some were bothered that on one of my many visits to their hideaway I had taken along a camera and photographed them — with their permission, of course — to send the pictures to Cairo. In Cairo, two periodicals were then published, one for the Allies and one purely in Greek. To boost the morale of the soldiers, they published photos of guerrilla groups in the countryside with their leaders. Some believed that I did this with the intent of harming them, by showing their faces and giving information about their numbers and the weapons they possessed.

Few of the truly capable representatives were lucky enough to escape then. From among the victims, I felt most sorry for the most honorable Greek military officer whom I had met, the dismissed Venizelist Colonel Giorgos Stathatos. He was a genuine soldier and a true patriot who had nothing to do with politics or politicians. He was loved by all in Didymoteichon and Orestiada, where he had spent a significant portion of his military service. Openhearted, compassionate and humorous, he did not at first understand subservience to the British and the consulate. However, he was able to withdraw quickly and return to the mountains. There, Karabekir's collaborator, Vassiliades — one of Odysseus' aides-de-camp, who moved among guerrillas though no one yet suspected the double role he was playing — set him a trap by having him write a letter to Kampalouris asking for aid and weapons in order to outfit the illiterate guerrillas and then, with their confidence, put together a new guerrilla group. He convinced him that he would be deceiving the British with Stathatos' prestige and they would then seize the weapons themselves.

Stathatos hesitated. Apparently, in his defense before the guerrilla tribunal after he was caught with the letter in his pocket, because he did not like this type of deception but was faced with Vassiliades' insistence (who he had instructions to eradicate as soon as possible, because with his knowledge and experience made him the only one to know enough about war to guide the ignorant guerrillas), he had backed down in the belief he was doing good. Stalwart to the end, he stood in tears before his executioners and refused to name Vassiliades. This is how a brave and pure patriot was lost and a traitor survived. It was the tactics of the Englishmen that caused the discord and division among them to reach this point.

The Plan to Send the SO Begins

My first concern was to make contact with the guerrillas. I met them on a small river island in Evros, known to the locals as Argyrohori. This was just outside Nea Vyssa, quite close to the border. The small island served as a passage point that at the same time provided security, isolated as it was with river water around it. It was here that ELAS had established a base for meetings with its couriers, who went back and forth to Turkey, and for new members who wanted to join ELAS.

I, too, was using the island as my base. It suited me well to meet there with villagers from the surrounding hamlets, since they cultivated corn there and fished in Evros. Indeed, because of my translator Valasidis, who they considered a hero, they loved the Americans and greeted me from afar as I approached.

They would wave their hands in the air and shout, "Welcome, Alekos the American!" I would return the greeting and gesture to them to inquire if the catch had been good. They would laugh and indicate a reply with their fingers, showing me they had caught, say, two or more fish.

I went to the island with Valasidis in order to meet with the guerrillas and to seek their help in cooperating with the SO mission. Naturally, they did not refuse. However, they said it would take time and that we would need to go to their headquarters, the location of which, for reasons of security, was never fixed. Time was also needed in order to develop our safe arrival there. A few days later, once everything had been organized to the last detail, we set off with Valasidis late in the evening. Along our route we encountered lookouts. Each would deliver us to the next until we reached Soufli. There, matters were difficult as the region was overseen by a sizable German force. However, they had provided for this, too: three horses were waiting for us, one for each of us and a third for the guard who would accompany us to the next watchman. Once again, the organization of these ordinary people truly impressed me.

Initially, we traveled next to the river. But from a certain point onward, we had to enter the cold current of water on horseback. As I was unaccustomed to riding, and even less so in water, I was having a rough time of it, but managed. After an absolutely freezing hour, we at last set foot on dry land. On our way, we met the sheepfold of Karakatsanis. Within it a marvelous fire was burning, which was precisely what we needed at that moment.

C o p y

Dear Roger:

Now that the excitement is somewhat out of the atmosphere hereabouts I shall give you a few lines, telling you my personal ideas about present plans. Complete story of conditions you shall get from reports.

Everyone concerned were very happy when cables came from Cairo. Jim left early this morning and good old ███ went with him to speed him up and fix a courier system from the south so messages to and from can come faster and save the mo vement of too many men over the border, which is pregnant with a lot of danger on one hand and diplomatic trouble between the Germans and Turkey. The later, if it comes at this time would certainly cause us a lot of hardship. After all ███ does not run the country.

It certainly is too bad the kids have so much trouble with radio contacts. Poor kids did not get a chance to iron out all difficulties before the crisis came. I feel sure when I go up with some new batteries and a few other things we shall be able to get on the beam.

It is hard to tell what the Huns have in mind to do. The first battle was not bad, though the people of that village will, undoubtedly pay pretty heavily but such is the way of war. I feel very confident that the new ███ leadership shall be able to cope with situation if given a little support from us, which I feel sure is forthcoming. These men are pretty cool and are people who have had several such and worse storms to weather before. Our boys, too, will settle down after their baptism and will come through in good fashion.

The goods at Boston will also be untangled, I hope, so we can get them up to them. That will help, I believe, with ███ help I can have a depot base at mouth of Evro as originally stated by me to you at Dover but hands are tied now and must wait for further developments.

Well, the most I can say is, that I am going to do whatever possible, under the circumstances. Many times, I wish I was a general or perhaps a civilian. Never knew rank counted so much but know now. It is brought home so much by other people. Too bad I am too old or I would have developed a terrific inferiority complex, a good costumer for Adler but no danger now.

Hope things clear up and we are left alone once more to do our little, in our way, unobstructed by meddling.

My opinion is that the ███ should at any cost avoid open season for the Huns and try to keep on the defensive at all times and so suggested to ███ and Jim, of course just in a personal advise way. I think ███ are of same opinion.

Think I covered all I can now remember. Until next time.

I shall remain sincerely,

ALEKKO

P.S. My best regards to McBaine & Mocarsky

APPROVED FOR RELEASE
Date ___________

B-34

A copy of Georgiades' letter drafted the same day the Kellis team crossed the Evros into Greek territory. He voices his disquiet concerning deficient training of the radio operators who participated in the mission, and attempts to predict the Germans' next moves in the region. From here onward, he uses the word "Ounoi" (Huns) instead of "Germans."

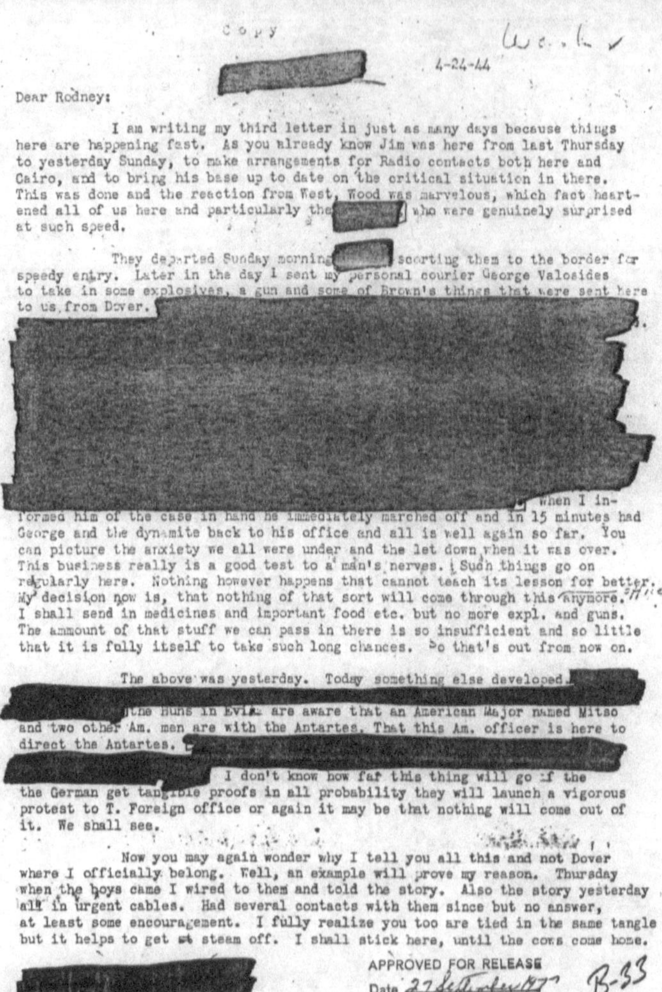

Copy of a letter to his supervisor Rodney Young taken from the
CIA declassified folders detailing the penetration of the Evros
region by the Kellis-led group of saboteurs. Main points cited
in the letter remain secret and have been redacted. In his letter,
Georgiades underlines Kellis' arrogant behavior which could harm
the goals of the Evros mission if Georgiades had not disregarded
his personal resentment and irascibility (dd. April, 24, 1944).

The mountain rancher welcomed us. Clearly, it was not the first time he had helped guerrillas. We dried our clothes, had warm milk with bread and on foot resumed toward our destination: the guerrilla headquarters just outside of Lefkimi.

When we arrived, it was daybreak.

The first thing I felt upon arriving at the Lefkimi camp was an indescribable iciness. It must have been the central camp of the 81st regiment of ELAS, as it had a large force of men. I was seeing many of them for the first time.

I heard the voice of Moravas, "Hello, Alekos!" I turned my head to see where the voice was coming from and saw him approaching me sullenly.

With his hand, he gestured for me to follow him a few meters further down. There, in an opening of a cave formed of natural rock, I saw an unknown man sitting.

"The comrade is from Thessaloniki," Moravas said. "They learned that matters had gotten out of control and sent him to put things in order."

He stood up, extended his hand and introduced himself, saying, "Athinodoros Katsavounidis. I know about you," he added. "Tell me how you want us to cooperate from now on."

Although I understood that I shouldn't ask too many questions, I did ask, "In the end, what happened to Odysseus?"

There was silence. Then, Moravas grabbed me by the hand, saying, "I'll explain it to you later."

What I heard afterwards left me literally speechless. Odysseus had been executed by his own comrades, the very ones that revered him, following a trial that Tiacas presided over, in the presence of 1,500 persons in Lefkimi Square. They had also invited me to attend the proceedings but, when we were crossing the river by boat, we came under fire and were forced to return to Turkey. When we finally managed to cross over on the night of February 7th, the trial was over, and Odysseus had been executed. The central leadership in Thessaloniki sent Katsavounidis to put things in order. He was a 25-year-old well-lettered communist from Pherai who had been exiled by Metaxas and who had genuine party papers.

The decision spoke of Odysseus' "unjustified extremist action" that had turned the local community against EAM, irreparably damaging the movement.

I also learned that in his last words to his comrades before being executed he warned them of new hardships if some people did not wise up in order to understand who Greece's real enemy was.

"I am dying for reasons which you will live to regret," he said, as if to prophesy what would follow, and continued before the weapons were fired: "The British and their Greek grovellers are responsible for the country's condition today. They are worse enemies than the Germans!"

Odysseus' role remained an enigma that no one, to my knowledge, has been able to solve. Some said he was a Bulgarian agent and that in March 1943 he had killed the EAM envoy to Evros before arriving at his intended station and appeared in his place. In any case, after Odysseus was executed, gold bars and a quantity of hashish were found concealed among his belongings.

These developments did not merely trouble me, they also worried me. They came at an extremely critical moment, on the eve of a major operation, and I could not tell what consequences the changes in guerrilla leadership might present. The newly appointed leader was a teacher, Lambros Kanakaris. The military authority was Kritonas, who was none other than Vangelis Kasapis, a thirty-year-old blacksmith by trade. His aide was Mimis Bayiotis. I knew them all and thought it positive that they knew me well, too. Of course, after the affair with the photographs I took at their hideaway a couple of months earlier, Kritonas was still guarded towards me and never hid it.

I stayed with them only one day. The atmosphere was already very heavy. Time, too, was pressing. It was now March 1944 and Kellis, who had already arrived in Istanbul in November, kept complaining that we were dawdling. I also had three days of travel ahead. That was how long the trip there had taken and the return would be as long.

I told them about the SO mission. They were enthusiastic and appeared long since ready to take part in the operation. They believed it to be inevitable that we would arm them and that they would at last obtain the weapons they lacked for their men.

I assembled my escorts and we took to the road to return to Adrianople. I made sure to finish a few pending urgent matters and gave Mavris instructions to finish off those I didn't have time to deal with myself. At that time, Kellis' mission and safe passage into Greek territory were absolute priorities. The real difficulties were just beginning.

The Bosporus bridge as Georgiades pictured the same day he traveled to
Istanbul in order to pick the members of Chicago Mission under James Kellis.

Cairo Grants Approval

I informed my Service in Cairo about developments in Evros. I asked for approval from Amoss before receiving Kellis and his team from Istanbul and he agreed. Even in Cairo, I am certain, they would have been distressed about the latest events, but we really were going all out and there was no time to waste, not by a long shot.

Meanwhile, the time had finally come for me to openly raise the British question on my own. Did my Service know that they disregarded and heaped contempt on each and every one of us, while secretly operating behind our backs, despite the Roosevelt-Churchill deal, in Ipsala where their crony Karabekir had his abode? And that they were arming the so-called nationalists to attack the EAM? Yes, that's right, the very same ones we were trying to get to work with us for the success of the SO mission. I imparted information that was thoroughly cross-checked, from firsthand sources, straight from the mouth of the officer responsible for my security officer, Sahin Targin. Information could not have been better validated than this.

This clearly proved effective. Recommendations were finally made to the British and, for instance, Demertzis, who was their man, was put on ice for a few months.

Thus resolved, and with freer reign, I departed for Istanbul on March 23rd to collect the SO team who had been waiting there since December. Kellis was fuming. He held me responsible for the delays, but I did not take it personally and I let it fall by the wayside. That was a pity because I later learned that he harbored an unjustified hatred toward me. And to think after I had acknowledged in him so many qualities, this left me with a bitter taste. But in this specific service, and particularly under the circumstances, bitterness among us was not an option and so I took care to put it behind me. Deep within me it had become clear that, under those conditions, ambition combined with selfishness and arrogance could destroy everything, including, of course, oneself.

At the end of March 1944, we set off from Adrianople for Evros, with a first stop at Uzun Köprü. There, we were to meet a Turkish officer with eight soldiers who would guide us up to the border. Our second stop was Saranli, a village on Turkish soil. We traveled through the night on horseback. In pitch black darkness, one could see nothing in the vicinity and a mix of snow and rain fell incessantly. We were chilled to the bone. At some point, Kaponis felt poorly and Kellis told me to ask the Turkish officer to stop. But he was uncompromising. His orders were not to stop anywhere for any reason until we reached our destination. We reached Saranli around midnight. We were awaited at the mayor's house. Exhausted, we drank hot tea and all fell to the floor to sleep. The Turks slept in an adjoining room.

The next morning, the freezing rain had stopped, so we were able to briefly go out into the yard to stretch. Kellis seemed quite anxious and on edge.

"Alex," he said, "are you certain your men understood we expect them today and not next year?" he asked in an acutely ironical tone because my couriers were late to appear and there was no way the team could go forward without them. True to form, for security reasons, they would lead, we would follow.

I had even asked them to secure for us a boat to cross the river, so as not to become soaked again. Another night passed. On the following morning, they finally appeared. Though the time was prohibitive, since the light of day left us exposed to unwanted gazes, Kellis insisted that we delay no further and so somewhere around ten or eleven o'clock in the morning we found ourselves, like deranged tourists, setting sail in the waters of the River Evros. We must have had not only guardian angels but God himself with us.

In a short while, we set foot in Greece. They led us to Laina, a small village nearby. We ate from the food they had prepared for us and we stayed waiting for the cart and mules to be loaded with the team's equipment. We loaded up and, as we prepared to mount our horses and set off for Lefkimi to find the guerrillas, one of our sentinels appeared, red-faced and short-winded from running.

"Stay here!" he warned. "As the cart entered the village, a car with four Germans appeared and stopped at the cafe on the square."

The hapless chap was panicky. We reentered the house and pulled back the horses, so as not to be seen from the road and draw attention.

Kellis had just begun to realize he was in a real battlefield, and this was not an exercise on paper. I saw him from the corner of my eye, and he did not fool me. He was afraid.

After an hour, which seemed like an eternity, a different sentinel arrived to tell us that the cart, meanwhile, quite literally, had passed under the noses of the Germans who, sitting in the sunshine, had seen it pass them by. Now it was already on its way to the mountain, with its load covered in straw.

We took deep breaths of relief, mounted our horses and departed for Lefkimi. At two o'clock in the afternoon, we were at the village square. The residents, who were notified of our arrival, had prepared a warm reception for us. Our feelings could not be concealed. For security reasons, we were split up in surrounding houses to sleep, where they had spread out the best bedding they had with spotless sheets. The next morning, we would get to work.

In the beginning, I remained with them to see how well their cooperation developed and whether I might be useful somehow. What troubled me most, while watching Kellis and the contentious way he reacted when things did not go precisely as he wished, was that perhaps they would have an altercation. These fellows, however, overlooked lost tempers and raised voices. They may not have gone to college and some might have had no schooling at all, but they were upright and straightforward. And as for giving their word, they meant what they said.

Another reason I remained there was there had been new changes in leadership in less than a month. This time, the young political leader was a young man, Lambros, Aris remained the military leader and Kritonas was chief captain.

Finally, seeing that things were going well and that a chemistry developed quickly between them, I left for Adrianople. The operation would be delayed a bit longer because they were waiting for Athens, the demolitions officer, to come from our base at Çeşme. They would arrive by sea carrying weapons and ammunition.

Explosives, weapons and ammunition were conveyed by airdrops. American airplanes stationed at Bari, Italy, flew in low at night and unloaded their cargo disassembled, as a precaution against materiel falling into the wrong hands.

Meanwhile, the guerrillas gathered together their forces from scattered camps nearby and sought to find new volunteers. At last, they had weapons. Athens alone, arriving with the Saint John, a caique, after sailing across the Aegean, brought with him 250 rifles, an equal number of light machine-guns and 11 heavy machine-guns. In just a few days, about one thousand people had joined the ranks of ELAS, including about ten former Greek Army officers. Our side trained intensively in the use of weapons for five days. And as it seems, they were successful. All American equipment was to remain in their possession afterwards, on one condition: that it was used only against the Germans and the Bulgarians.

The targets of the Kellis mission, which was code-named "Chicago," were two bridges at Svilengrad and Alexandroupolis. The first was code-named "Milwaukee," the second was "Joliet." My suggestion to target the Python bridge instead was not, for some reason, approved by headquarters in Cairo. Obviously, there were factors I had not considered. However, I was correct in my evaluation that the Germans would be able to quickly rebuild the two bridges. With one difference: the new ones could not bear heavy loads and the flow of raw materials came sharply to a halt shortly afterward. So much so that 690 loads of ore already purchased by Germany stayed idle at the stations of the two cities, awaiting the green light for passage by sections. In the end, they stayed there until the end of the war.

Brazeness that almost came at a high cost

After so many years, I am still overcome by panic at the mere thought of what could have happened that Easter Sunday, a month before the sabotage, if the Germans had succeeded in setting up an ambush as Kellis' team and the guerrillas were celebrating Greek Easter at Lefkimi.

But I need to pick up the thread at an earlier point.

After I led Kellis and his two companions to the hideaway at Lefkimi and I saw that their cooperation with Athinodoros, Kritonas and the others progressed well, I returned to Adrianople. Not too many days had passed when all of a sudden, outside the house I was using as a base, an official vehicle stopped with two Turkish officers, Sahin and Kellis. He was a sight — nearly unrecognizable, exhausted and in a poor condition. As if ashamed, he hurriedly made his way to the room that he had used before leaving and shook the supervisor's hand with a hasty "thank you."

I avoided asking the Turks what had happened. They may have thought I already knew. I thanked them in turn and closed the door.

I spent quite some time in the dark, as it was already nightfall. There was no sound from within the room. I wondered what he might be doing. Was he asleep? The light, however, was off. I would have noticed it from beneath the door.

At some point while I was working, I heard the door open and James slowly approached my desk. He took a seat without asking and for the first time I saw him smoking.

"I see you've picked up some of their bad habits while up there," I said jokingly in an attempt to lighten up the situation. I understood that something serious had happened and that he was finding it difficult to begin telling me about it.

He seemed frazzled. Nothing about him was at all reminiscent of the arrogant behavior of his initial appearance. In hindsight, and from all that he said to me, I realized that he felt guilty for getting carried away by the locals and taking his group, all dressed in their American military uniforms, to the church on Easter Sunday.

"Alex," he said, "it seems some people in the village set us up." He began speaking slowly at first, then continued: "You had to be there to see the battle that broke out. At some point, I thought to myself that all was finished. We scattered to avoid being caught. They took us in different directions, running along the small streets of the village. I don't know what happened to the others. We couldn't even use the wireless. The Germans would have found us. Eventually they led us to a hill from where we watched the battle, which lasted until daybreak. The next day, we assembled at the hideaway to assess the situation. The guerrillas had been left without ammunition and needed reinforcements quickly. They feared German retaliations. Kritonas asked me to send a message to Cairo and to come here with my escorts to alert you, to inform your liaison in Istanbul and Amoss in Cairo that things are getting tough, and the situation is really serious."

"How do you think it happened?" I asked.

"Look, it surely was no coincidence that one hundred Germans appeared in the village at night and began strafing. Someone who saw us at the church must've betrayed us. It was my fault to make our presence a target. It seemed like we were making a show of strength. On such a day, with the whole village at the church, how can anyone know what others were thinking?"

He took a long drag on his cigarette and fixed his gaze at a remote point for a while.

"It was ridiculous," he continued. "After the revelry and food, with the roast lambs and the wine we drank, we fell sound asleep. They woke us abruptly in the middle of the night to get us out. In the dark, we couldn't see what we were wearing. Some grabbed the clothes of the others. But what impressed me was the equanimity of the Greeks. Such stalwarts, they were. Regardless of its unfortunate outcome, I'll never forget this Easter. We've never lived such moments in America. Here, the people truly celebrate these days. Imagine if there hadn't been a war going on."

Two decades passed before I learned what had happened then. It was in the early 1960s, while I was in Athens, when Kritonas sent me manuscripts from Sofia, where as a political refugee he had sought refuge after the civil war, to ask me for help to get them published. We failed to do so, however. In Greece because he wrote what he wrote, and spirits had not yet calmed; in Bulgaria because of his criticism of the communists at the time.

Before the Attack

The problem of ELAS was weapons. It was their main demand during our initial meeting in September 1943. I explained then that I understood how serious this issue was, but that my mission was different. I could cover a series of other needs for them, such as medicine, clothing, trafficking of illegal press and even money, but under no circumstances would I be the one to provide them with arms. I could only promise to convey their wishes to Cairo. And that I did. Nearly six months went by without a response, in part because of Odysseus' terrorist tactics. Then, Kellis' team of American saboteurs made their appearance.

The news spread like lightning and raised the morale of the people of Evros. On March 8, Farfaras and Moravas delivered a communiqué from the new leadership which sought to cooperate with us on a new basis. And so it happened.

In that meeting, however, the ELAS guerrillas seemed disappointed with the small number of weapons promised to them by Kellis. The deal was about to founder had I not urged both sides to avoid losing the opportunity of cooperating at this critical time.

Finally, on March 10, the two sides came to terms. In fact, they signed a type of protocol and from that moment the 81st Regiment of ELAS was considered a component of the Allied Forces Headquarters Middle East. A few days afterward, they organized the hideaway of the American mission. Part of the agreement was to provide information, passed on to me, about the movements of the Germans in the region and in neighboring Bulgaria. Kellis would provide them with 600 long rifles, 200 semiautomatics and 8 heavy machine guns. But the main achievement of that bargain was mutual trust. And our side came to understand that they were dealing with fighters and honest people who, with no personal interest, cared only to drive the occupiers out of their country — and were ready to defy hunger, cold and even danger — to their families in the cities.

For Kellis, coordination with them was a tremendous lesson because the climate of terrorism under Odysseus had given Cairo the impression that Thrace had been transformed into a slaughterhouse. That was certainly the reason why, for so many months, they were reluctant to send arms to the guerrillas. But most of all, Kellis and his team were thrilled by the welcome of the crowd at the church on Easter Sunday and by the feast and revelry in the village square.

"Long live the Americans!"

"Long live the Allies!"

"We want weapons!"

"Death to fascism, freedom for the people!"

The crowd roared and girls tossed flowers at Kellis, Mike and Gus. They gave them red eggs, followed by an awe-inspiring dance. Kritonas then took them by horseback to the neighboring village of Trifylli, where the locals had arranged festivities. Again, there resonated cries of joy and slogans about freedom and the Americans, who, in their eyes, had come to these parts as liberators. They took them down from the horses and carried them throughout the village on their shoulders. There followed a wild feast which continued back to Lefkimi. Literally stumbling from wine and distilled grape wine they had been offered, they fell into a deep sleep — only to be madly awakened by the sounds of gunfire from the guerrilla sentries as they saw the German forces approach the village.

Who had betrayed them? Kellis? That is to say, all of us? These thoughts tormented us for years. It took us three decades to discover, by reading the manuscripts of Kritonas, that he had organized it on his own to show the Americans the fervor with which the guerrillas fought, the foreign occupier. And that they truly needed weapons as soon as possible. Of course, there was great risk with enormous consequence, including, especially, the failure of the "Chicago" mission. This was rescued by the guerrillas and ended up on the hill of Aghios Thanasis from where it dispersed as the Germans, a force of two battalions, had since settled in Lefkimi.

In that battle, no guerrilla was killed, unlike the Germans who, we learned, had many victims.

Unfortunately, the mentality was altogether foreign to us, despite the Greek blood in our veins. It was difficult for us to vindicate when so much suspicion existed against us. And this became clear on another occasion. As Kellis told me, at one point during the Lefkimi celebrations with the roast lamb and dancing, he turned to Kritonas and said, "Pity we didn't bring a camera with us. Such revelry should be shown to our own back in America."

Then he responded, "At least you, Jimmy," —as he called him—"would take them for a good cause. But as for Alekos, I very much doubt he was taking them for magazines, like he said, published in Cairo, and we showed that we believed him… Tell me, truly. What do you know? That's why he was photographing us? Or did he want to count us and show where we were?"

That same night, after the battle with the Germans, Kritonas gave him a second test. He asked him to write, in his own hand, a message to Cairo with instructions to immediately send the weapons, since these people were not criminals but honest patriots. Also, that their ammunition had been spent in the battle with the Germans and from that point onward the people of Lefkimi were exposed to reprisals by the Germans and remained defenseless.

Indeed, Kellis did exactly that. His verbatim message said: "On second day of Easter, morning hours, a two-battalion German force moved against the rebel headquarters at Lefkimi STOP Fighting heroically, rebels repulsed the German attack, causing serious losses with dead and injured STOP Night hours, ammunition depleted STOP Immediately need supply of weapons and ammunition STOP Expect for German losses retaliation against defenseless Lefkimi civilians and rebel families STOP Delayed supply places our lives in jeopardy and effects prestige of American flag STOP We confirm guerrillas are not criminals but ardent patriots and fanatical supporters of allied cause STOP"

Kellis confided to me, after they arrived at Adrianople, that after sending a second telegram to Cairo Kritonas asked him to visit the "hornet's nest." He had given this name to the Greek consulate because British Intelligence agents had set up there and he would speak coarsely to them — and even curse them, if necessary — for the misinformation they sent to Allied headquarters that effectively prevented arms shipments to the guerrillas.

"Listen, Jimmy," he said before leaving. "It's sure Turkish border guards heard the gunfire. That lasted a whole day, so it wasn't something minor. Everybody will want to hear from you what happened. There, you need to put your foot down and tell them how bravely we fought and what damage we caused to the Germans. Oh, and tell a little lie, too, that the Germans already began to retaliate — that's nothing terrible. Even if they didn't do so until now, nothing prevents them now that you're absent. Their tactics are known."

Seeing that James was hesitant, Kritonas said: "I understand your American upbringing doesn't let you scheme and be sly, but, Jimmy, doesn't the Greek blood in your veins make any difference? What the hell, my friend, can't you see it won't happen differently and that they need to be pressured to send us weapons? After all, all lies aren't bad. There are also those told for a good cause."

In the end, Kellis was persuaded to send a second telegram from our base that read: "Traveled to Turkish territory, our Adrianople base STOP Total lack of ammunition worsens guerrilla situation dramatically STOP Germans intensify retaliations STOP My mission prestige and American nation are shattered in guerrilla perceptions if weapons not shipped immediately STOP Rebel indignation poses risk to my life STOP My return to mountains unneeded without weapons STOP Fate of my team members depends on sending weapons STOP"

Despite the fact that Kellis went along with Kritonas, suspicion existed. How else to interpret the requirement from the latter?

"Jimmy, in your meetings with them, I want you to have Panos and Moravas with you."

Was there any doubt that, before leaving, he had given instructions to both his escorts?

Some days passed before James returned to the mountains on April 26. He brought good news. In the meantime, the guerrillas were anxious and continually asking Mike and Gus how they viewed matters and whether their leader could persuade his superiors about the situation prevailing in their region. Their joy when they saw him arriving — and as they could read on his face the news he brought before he even opened his mouth — was beyond description.

The Big Day Finally Arrives

The plan Kellis laid out was this: he, along with Athens, 170 rebels and 700 kilos of explosives, would strike the bridge at Svilengrad along the Greek-Bulgarian border. In simultaneous coordination, the marine Thomas Curtis, together with Mike Angelos, 50 guerrillas and 250 kilos of explosives, would strike, within Greek territory, the bridge outside Alexandroupolis. By that time, around 135,000 tons of chromium had passed through the Danube and/or via both bridges, about ten itineraries per day that also transported passengers to Berlin.

It took two days for Kellis and his men to march up the mountains, zig-zagging all the way to hide their tracks. The locals helped them avoid Bulgarian and German lookouts. Eventually, on May 27 they approached their goal and hid. Kellis and Athens and two guerrillas began to reconnoiter the area. They counted a total of 10 German and 21 Bulgarian guards. For the while they stayed under the bridge, they could appreciate the importance of the Allied decision to destroy it. It was quite tall and 210 feet long. They were able to count 283 cargo wagons, apparently destined for Berlin, and among them two passenger wagons.

Two days later, on May 29, Kellis gathered them for final briefings. Everyone was at peak morale and could hardly wait to celebrate. He explained the plan in detail and what each member was to do. He then sent out a group of scouts with orders to prevent chance arrivals of reinforcements. Once everything and everyone was ready, the strike group cut the communication lines. It was around 11 PM.

According to the plan, he would place the explosives in the bridge's superstructure and Athens would do the same at the base. Not a sound was heard throughout the entire process. At 12:10, precisely when all was ready after exactly eighty minutes and the slow-burning fuse was lit, the Germans caught wind that something was going on, fired a flare to locate the saboteurs and shot into the air with automatic weapons. But it was already too late. The bridge had already collapsed in huge pieces.

Both Kellis and Athens observed it as they moved off to meet up with the others at the agreed rendezvous point. From there, they followed an escape route via the Arda river. Somewhere around four o'clock in the morning, they encountered a German patrol and called for reinforcements. Kellis, Athens and the rest of the team pulled forward and the guerrillas stayed behind to stop the Germans. The chase went on for three days and the battle was quite rough. The German commanding officer, a major, was killed as were many of his men; of the guerrillas, not one.

Late in the evening on the very next day, Mike Angelos encountered a Greek police officer guarding the vicinity as he walked under the bridge on the Greek side. When the police officer asked him who he was and what he was doing there at such an hour, he simply replied, "I'm an American. I came to demolish the bridge."

A smile instantly brightened the police officer's face as he asked what he could do to help him.

"Careful, though," he said in warning to Curtis as he shuffled down in descent from the hillock. "I'm not at all sure the rest of us guarding here will be kind and willing to help you."

By the time he descended, Curtis and his men had already encircled the guards' quarters. Twenty-five of them came to their side and only five who feared for their families and the fate that might await them volunteered to be neutralized by being tied up to trees.

Shortly before midnight, Curtis blew up the bridge. The mission had been accomplished.

Ordered Back to Istanbul

In the interval between my return from the guerrilla hideaway and the unexpected appearance of Kellis accompanied by Turkish officers, I received orders to go to Istanbul. I arrived on March 3, 1944.

There, I learned that a problem had arisen with the staff of our base in Çesme. The base was then managed by the archaeologist John Caskey, from the University of Cincinnati, whose code name was "Chickadee" (bee-eater). Caskey had taken part in excavations in Troy. Then, for a decade until 1959, he was director of the American Archaeological School in Athens. He had been recruited, as had many of his other colleagues in the OSS, and had even taken part in the rescue of refugees with boats on the Alexandroupolis-Çesme route. But he was disappointed because he could not get the green light to load, along with the refugees, all the Jews of Thessaloniki who had fled there to avoid deportation to Auschwitz. And so they too were lost.

The reason for this was that Emniyet did not want them on their territory. Young avoided dealing with the Turkish authorities, embroiled in the difficult task of transporting women and children, preferring instead to send money to the Jews of Athens to find a way to save themselves. Young refused to back down even when US Consul General Burton Berry threatened in a state of fury to write to Roosevelt personally.

In the end, only 800 Jews from Northern Greece escaped and reached the Turkish coast, but not through our own actions. Today, we hear a lot about the tragic fate that befell those people and the many survivors who came to America to live in safety. But the fact remains that the US government did nothing to save them then. As bitter as this truth may be, it must be stated clearly so that everyone knows what the facts of the matters are. The Bulgarian Jews that I managed to help escape by bribing railway workers on Bulgarian soil, I did so without asking and waiting for official instructions, which would have wasted valuable time.

The day after my arrival, I met Sperling's assistant, Virginia Grace, code named "Tiggie." She too was an archaeologist, a New Yorker and Caskey's peer. Before the war, Grace had taken part in excavations in Pergamon and Cyprus. She asked me to tell her if I could take on both bases. My conversation with her was pleasant because she was direct, particularly intelligent and very dynamic.

John Caskey, an archaeologist with deep knowledge of the Greek
language, excavated Troy, and, after WWII, Lerna and Keos when he
was director of the Athens Archaeological School, from 1949-1959.
He and Elizabeth Caskey were assigned to the OSS Office at Çeşme
(Turkey). In 1943, he was instructed to facilitate the journey of
refugees from the port of Alexandroupolis to the Middle East. Homer
Davies, of the American College in Athens, which was closed during
the war, was put in charge of the Smyrna Office.

At this point, I must point out that the recruitment of archaeologists
to the OSS ranks was a truly astute decision by Donovan. Due to the
nature of their work, first of all, archaeologists are very observant. Then,
they spend most of their time in the countryside, looking and listening to
things that are impossible to learn in an office. Their trump card, however,

is their contact with the locals, whose trust they gain quickly and without suspicion by using their status as a cover.

One of them was the renowned archaeologist Nelson Gluck. With Rabbinic studies in Germany, Gluck took part in the excavations of the American School of Oriental Studies in Jerusalem that uncovered Solomon's mines. Having joined under Dr. Penrose, head of the Middle East General Administration, thanks to the cover provided by his profession, he managed to organize an amazing network of informers who brought news from the West Bank to the Allied Command in Cairo. Among the first items taught, of course, in the field of intelligence was that the British were involved in previous wars. We walked in their footsteps when we, the Americans, took our first steps to organize secret services under the adverse conditions of wartime.

Among the needs that had emerged was for direct and timely exploitation of the vast amounts of information that arrived daily. It was then that Donovan, based on experience from his brief term as Coordinator of Information in President Roosevelt's office, decided to order the creation of the Research and Analysis Division, staffed by experienced diplomats, lawyers, people from the banking sector, but mainly historians and archaeologists. The latter proved to be the most productive.

The American Archaeological School of Athens, Greece, is one of the oldest schools of classical studies. Under the code "Plover," the OSS recruited four of its outstanding executive directors, who, because of their bravery, were soon promoted to senior officers of the American military. I recall my friend and compatriot, Costas Couvaras, a journalist at New York's "National Herald" newspaper, who was also recruited by the OSS and participated in operations in Greece. He told me how, upon passing from Cairo via Çeşme into Greece, he was impressed by the skill and speed the archaeologists at base produced false passports and identity cards for those entering occupied Greece.

That period was perhaps the toughest for me because I was on the eve of a major sabotage operation, faced with changes in the EAM leadership in Evros, while at the same time trying to reassure everyone to stop fearing retaliations by Odysseus gang at the border, as Turks were no longer unwilling to accept more refugees on their territory.

Costas Couvaras, a journalist at New York's "National Herald" newspaper, recruited by OSS. He participated in several operations in Greece.

Moreover, Cairo was asking me to conduct penetrations on Bulgarian soil for intelligence gathering. Before I made a decision, however, I asked for time and went to Çesme in order to see things firsthand. It did not take much to understand that our base there was one of the most significant ones. It functioned as a transit facility, supplying us with food, medicines and war material of all sorts. Having understood its importance, and thus the time someone would need to dedicate for the base to function properly, I realized that it was impossible to manage both at the same time.

Thus, it was assigned to Homer Davis, director of the American College of Athens, which had been closed because of the war. After the war, I learned that Davis returned to Athens to continue his term. He retired there in 1960.

A Network of Double Agents is Exposed

When the case came to light, it shook everyone. Most of all those in Cairo and Washington who could, from their positions, appreciate the consequences of the conspiratorial activity of this network which had literally acted under our noses.

The root of all evil was in the appointment of that absurd Lanning Macfarland, from Chicago, in Spring 1943, to manage our base in Istanbul, which Sperling was operating on his own. Macfarland, an American of Irish descent, had voluntarily presented himself in Washington and requested to be sent as a volunteer to Yugoslavia because he knew persons and things and had learned a bit of the language during his time there as an ambulance driver during World War I. He was brought to Donovan, who, despite initial reservations, put Macfarland in contact with Lawrence Steinhardt, who had undertaken the Istanbul ambassadorship and was in Washington on official business.

The hasty decision to entrust Macfarland with this important position without vetting or training him was due to the critical contours of the situation in the Balkans and Eastern Europe. The governments of Bulgaria, Romania and Hungary were showing signs of fatigue and war-weariness and were primed for defection to the Allied side.

The gist of it was this: this man was quite simply unsuited for the job. Devoid of experience, he made a mess of things right from the outset. At that time, Istanbul was a veritable greenhouse for agents of all origins, due to its geographical position and Turkey's role, which ostensibly remained neutral while supporting the Axis.

Inside that bubbling cauldron of more than two hundred agents, everyone did everything they could to conceal their roles: some maintained their cover as journalists, others as professors and still others as businessmen in the dozens of businesses that had sprung up in the city. Macfarland, better known by his nickname of "Packy," made the rounds dressed as a spy, as if every day were Carnival or Halloween.

When he entered the Park Hotel lounge, the pianist would stop playing and then begin pounding the keys with a popular song of the era, "Boo, Boo, Baby, I'm A Spy!" When the damage was done and he was expelled from there, he defended himself by claiming the actions were deliberate: to deflect the attentions of Turkish counter-espionage, thereby allowing those who did the actual work to proceed unhindered, namely the journalists and professors at the American school, Robert College. As if he were in any position to fool the Emniyet by officially appearing in his capacity as the director of an American financial institution.

But even if his right-hand man was a complete drunkard, matters could not be worse. Whenever he entered a bar, he would greet the crowd in a loud voice, "Hail, spies!"

The Germans who had broken a British code and learned that their code name was "1200" would respond by shouting: "The land of '1200' greets you! The country of '1200' Über Alles!"

The British, for their part, being past masters at agent affairs, enjoyed gloating at our expense and mocked our lack of experience and naiveté.

Initially, in any case, Macfarland's idea to collaborate with the "Dogwood" network of Alfred Schwarz, a Jewish entrepreneur of Czech origin who had been in Istanbul since 1928, made a great impression on Washington, which asked for messages to be sent directly for analysis by a special OSS team Donovan set up there. With Schwarz' intervention, the British Intelligence Service accepted to cooperate with our Service and provide intelligence collection training. Very strict instructions were then given to dispel any and all implications that the State Department was aware of the network operating in Istanbul because this would cause great dismay to the Turks. Not that the latter did not know what was happening, of course. At that time, no foreigner who went to live in Istanbul was thought innocent or, at least, irrelevant. The Turks had eyes and ears everywhere. Along the most famous shopping street, the bustling Istiklal, even the lemonade sellers were informants.

Our people, who were based at the US Consulate, rented, for their convenience, an extra building on the Bosphorus. A photography workshop was created there, which was also where they held their meetings. In order to come into contact with the network, Schwarz opened a branch of the American company Western Electric. When various merchants and salesmen from the surrounding Balkan countries came there, they knowingly or unknowingly transferred valuable information on the situation in their countries of origin.

And while things developed speedily after Macfarland's cooperation with Schwarz and the "Dogwood" network, misleading information was deliberately passed onto the Allied camp that led to the bombardment of the wrong targets. This helped, initially, to expose the role of Otto von Hatz and afterward four others who were all members of the network and agents of the Germans.

Von Hatz was a young colonel in the Hungarian army who had served as a military attaché in Sofia and Ankara. His position, however, did not prevent him from switching to the Soviet camp when the Red Army entered his country.

It is a fact that things got off on the wrong foot. This was because of the Allies' haste to bring Hungary to their side, even in the last phases of the war. Because of that haste, Schwarz's demand, who also functioned as MI6 and hid behind the code-name of the organization, not to reveal his sources and his refusal to give data to crosscheck the identities of "Dogwood" members by the Intelligence Service was acknowledged as a calamitous error.

Yet, the role of agent "Dahlia," who was none other than an SS officer named Fritz Fiala, an avowed Nazi and press counselor of the German embassy, turned out to be the worst of all. As a journalist, Fiala had written a series of bespoke articles for Eichmann, in the most prominent of which he described Auschwitz as a camp with humane living conditions for its detainees. All "Dogwood" agents, behind which hid Schwarz himself, had flower pseudonyms, such as "Magnolia," "Hyacinth," "Lotus," "Begonia" and so forth.

At that time, the "Dogwood" network had 67 ancillary agents. Among them, two anti-Hitler German doctors, who worked for OSS as photographers, and some Turkish businessmen who, as couriers, transported messages via the diplomatic pouches of foreign embassies by buying-off and bribing their senders. The network's activity was so productive that, between December 1943 and February 1944, over 150 OSS reports based on "Dogwood" information were sent to Washington.

Macfarland appointed Archibald Coleman as a liaison with the OSS. He was a well-trained officer and experienced in unmasking agents. He had, however, failed in his previous assignments because he was himself exposed: once in Mexico and a second time in Spain, where he got orders for immediate transfer in July 1942. Coleman had the code-name "Cereus" and was officially represented as a correspondent for *The Evening Post*. He arrived in Istanbul a year after Macfarland, at the critical point when operation "Sparrow" began and three OSS parachutists with instructions from Cairo to set foot on Hungarian territory. The head of the OSS in Cairo was Lada Valerian Mocarski, a colonel. Mocarski was a Russian émigré, the son of a tsarist Russian general who escaped abroad when the Bolshevik revolution broke out. His greatest success as an OSS agent was noted when, leaving his post in Cairo, he teamed up with Allen Dulles in Europe and managed to penetrate Italian elite circles, getting hold of the diaries of Mussolini's foreign minister, Count Ciano.

Like Dulles, later the CIA's first director, Mocarski was on the board of directors for Schroeder Bank, of British interests. The tragedy was that the specific bank, along with other American interests, such as Socony Oil, had hired Eichmann himself as a salesman and did business in the 1920s and 1930s with Germany and Hitler, as did Averell Harriman, who introduced the Tyssen family to the German dictator. As is known, they undertook to support him financially.

The alarm was raised when it was revealed that there were double agents in the network and that British and American fighters had bombed the wrong targets. Mocarski asked Donovan to remove Macfarland immediately, to halve the base personnel and to install Frank Wisner as new head of base.

Eventually, the "Dogwood" network collapsed on July 31, 1944 and Macfarland left Turkey through Yugoslavia a week later, on August 9. No one in the OSS wanted to work with him after that because he was "burnt," as was often said about failed agents. Coleman was discharged and Schwarz was dismissed. The latter remained in Istanbul as an entrepreneur before finally returning to Switzerland.

Did the Suitcase with the Documents Lead to the Double Agents?

This question still torments me. Chronologically, the two incidents are related and my unforeseen promotion to the rank of captain may also be related to the event.

Things happened as follows: In those years, Bulgaria's irredentism was at its peak because of the Treaty of Neuilly-sur-Seine after the end of World War I, according to which Bulgaria had to forgo its demands in Western Thrace. Conditions, in fact, seemed very favorable for Bulgaria's dream of access to the Aegean, or the Belomorie, as the Bulgarians call it. After the concession of Macedonia and part of Greek Thrace, granted in return for cooperation with the Axis to facilitate the transit of troops from Germany to her territory, Bulgaria assumed that, this time, her outlet to the sea was guaranteed. For these reasons, Bulgaria had the green light from the Germans, who were in control of a zone in the Evros region from where loads of iron ore from Turkey were destined for the supplies of the Axis war machine on German, Austrian and Polish territory. To secure its presence in the region, Bulgaria engaged in raids, thefts and acts of incredible terrorism at the expense of the local Greek population. Indeed, beside the Germans' tolerance, the Bulgarian raiders benefited from the armed forces of the notorious Tsaus Anton. He had allied himself with Bulgarian fascists and from his base on Bulgarian soil decimated the lives and property of Greek housewives, many of whom were the victims of continuous slaughter by the *comitadjis*.

The rebels gave a resounding answer to that violence. The companies of the 81st ELAS Regiment of the Soufli-Trigona area were given orders to capture every Bulgarian who dared enter rebel-held areas and, in addition, to watch their movements in the frontier outposts, which they had abandoned after their advance to Greek territory, but which were still used for their raids when needed.

Their greatest success occurred on June 10, 1944, when the Soufli company managed to surprise and capture an entire force at one of the Bulgarian military outposts, totaling about twelve men, and confiscate their precious equipment of twenty-eight long rifles, five thousand bullets, about eighty grenades and two radiotelephones.

ELAS's tactic was to leave letters at the ambush-staging outposts, threatening retaliation on Bulgarian soil, even to the detriment of civilians, if the *comitadjis* did not stop their raids on Greek villages.

After ELAS seized a second outpost, the Bulgarians sent out a search airplane to locate and neutralize the rebels, but that proved impossible. They were thus held back until the Bulgarian robbery raids in Evros finally ended.

However, their cooperation with Greek quislings and the Germans continued with espionage against the Allies. The guerrillas managed to set up an ambush, just outside Orestiada, against the infamous Bulgarian general Kiroff. But due to a misfiring of a rebel's gun, he managed to escape. His confederate, however, a Greek traitor from Orestiada named Dinis was killed.

Two Bulgarian-speaking villagers from Dikaia, who worked for Kiroff, were also caught. One, a Turkish teacher, whose trademark were his red hair and long beard, tried to cross the border to escape. He threw his suitcase. The guerrillas allowed him to leave, but confiscated the precious cargo he carried, which proved to belong to Kiroff. The suitcase was filled with documents, all in Turkish, except for one letter written in English. I do not remember the name of the author, but I remember he wrote that he was worried about the health of Alexandra's daughter, who lived in New York.

The rebels gave the suitcase to Sahin on condition that it was delivered to me. In turn, I forwarded it to Sperling, my chief of station since I instantly appreciated the importance of its contents. It was full of codes and names of Turkish agents acting on behalf of the Germans and against the Allies, using as a cover different identities in the vast market of Istanbul. As a result of this revelation, the Turks recalled twenty of their own agents from Bulgaria. Some of them were executed.

Shortly after the suitcase arrived in Cairo, I was promoted to the rank of captain. This case proved to be quite significant and was regarded as a personal achievement when I was awarded the Legion of Merit.

I do not think it at all improbable that the contents of this suitcase caused the collapse of the "Dogwood" network and the removal of Macfarland from the Istanbul base. In retrospect, of course, various interpretations of the case were written because it became fertile ground for all sorts of theories. But none took into account how the suitcase with its precious secrets fell into our hands: it did not happen on a moving train with Americans who managed to stop German intelligence agents traveling to Berlin, nor did it occur as a result of double agents, working for us or MI6, being exposed.

Still, these things happen — and not only under wartime conditions.

Change of Guard:
Frank Wisner Succeeds Macfarland

With the removal of Macfarland, who became head for the evacuation of Allied pilots held hostage on Serb territory, the Istanbul Office was given a new liaison with Cairo on Donovan's orders: Frank Wisner, a Wall Street attorney, more or less my age, who enlisted in the US Navy shortly after the attack on Pearl Harbor. He was originally assigned to the OSS Office in Bucharest. One of his successes was having persuaded King Michael to allow the escape of a number of American airmen being held as prisoners of war. Wisner's hatred toward Russia, however, became an obsession. Watching the advance of Soviet troops in the countries of Southeastern Europe, he felt great disquiet and saw that America would soon face a new enemy.

Wisner was among those who remained in the CIA after the end of the war. He was promoted to Deputy Director of Plans, a successor to Dulles, but he had an inglorious end. He himself was a victim of the Cold War climate of the era as he faced Hoover's accusations that his lover during the war years, Princess Karatza, was an agent of the Soviets. But furthermore, events, such as the suppression of the Hungarian revolution in 1956 by the Soviet army, resulted in a deterioration of his health, bringing about manic-depressive symptoms that required hospitalization for six months in a psychiatric clinic. He returned to the service after a few years and Dulles assigned him as chief of station in London where he worked with Philby. His state of health deteriorated, however, and in 1961 he was asked to resign. He committed suicide in October 1965.

Upon his arrival in Istanbul, I was instructed to visit him and I must say that in our conversation he showed himself to be a quite imperturbable person. He asked me if I was able and willing to penetrate Bulgaria and Romania for intelligence gathering and, naturally, I said that I would have no objections as long as I had the means and proper connections and, of course, the approval of Cairo. He was pleased with my answer.

Suddenly, there was a silence which he broke himself by asking, "Alex, what's your rank?" My answer left him speechless.

"It sounds incredible! Please, go to our embassy in Ankara tomorrow. I'll instruct our military attaché to promote you to a higher rank."

He looked at me again to make sure I was not fooling with him. He tossed down on the desk before him a sheaf of papers he had held in his hands and said, "It's not possible!"

The next day, I actually took the train to Ankara. I was supposed to meet someone named George Earle, who was our naval attaché there, but in the end I met his successor.

Earle… What a story he was. The only thing I learned then was that he had come to Turkey from Sofia in a rather adverse transfer because he was an alcoholic and had caused a string of scandals during his tenure. We all wanted to learn what happened to one another and how things had worked out after returning home. But what I learned about him after the war exceeded even my wildest imagination. All the more so for me, being a simple man, a Pittsburgh provincial who struggled hard to survive and study. Earle's story was one of pampering, with powerful connections that reached even to President Roosevelt himself. The son of a family of wealthy sugar industrialists from Pennsylvania… it truly resembled a novel.

From birth, Earle was a special case: eccentric in behavior with an imposing presence; stout, blond, with rich wavy hair and deep blue eyes; permanently drunk and a loud talker; abandoned Harvard for the Navy; forsook family traditions that placed his ancestors — among them, American founding father, Benjamin Franklin — firmly in the Republican camp; and the first governor with the Pennsylvania Democratic Party elected at the age of forty-five. He could even have been nominated for the US presidency, but corruption scandals and alcoholism got in the way of his aspirations. He resigned early to claim a seat in the Senate and went to see Roosevelt, who seemed to have a high regard of him because of his exuberant character, to ask him for a place post in Europe. And he sent him as an ambassador to Sofia.

His turbulent life there — with endless parties, drinks and mistresses, among them a beautiful Hungarian singer, Adrienne Molnár, who refused to follow him to Istanbul until the Germans used her as bait, hoping to intercept his official secrets — of course, does not fit into a single book. However, it is a fact that he had managed, by his lifestyle, to become a real headache to the Nazis, creating innumerable incidents.

One such incident happened at a famous Sofia nightclub with two German secret agents, with whom he began a quarrel over the orchestra's song, ending up with Earle literally breaking a bottle of champagne over the head of one of them. The bizarre episode remains known as the "Balkan Bottle Battle." Eventually he left Sofia when Bulgaria declared war on America in December 1941, siding with the Axis. On his way back to Washington, he stopped in Casablanca and there met General Patton, also known for his explosive character. They warmed up to each other from the first moment. In Washington, he asked to see President Roosevelt. This time, he asked to be sent to Istanbul as assistant to the naval attaché of Ankara, assuring him that he was a personal friend to Steinhardt, and that they would get along fine. The President, who was known to enjoy chatting with him, immediately gave his approval.

In Istanbul, his place of residence would be the Park Hotel. But even upon arriving at the reception, before he could even make his way up to the expensive suite, he had already become the center of attention, not just because every day an entirely new caprice would become a matter of endless discussion.

He had with him a huge Great Dane and a parrot, which he needed to have in his bedroom. One serious disadvantage, however, that combined with his exuberant personality and became a real threat to himself and to the interests he served, was the absolute lack of security measures. He otherwise possessed exceeding intelligence and self-esteem. Regrettably, due to his behavior, these were not used to their full potential.

A characteristic example of this was when Roosevelt instructed him to examine research findings to determine who was behind the massacre of the Poles in Katyn. Earle rightly concluded that the Soviets were guilty, but no one took him seriously and his findings were tossed in the garbage. Indeed, the US President did not want this fact to be made public. At that time, such an accusation was far too serious for the two great powers fighting the same enemy: Nazism. Nothing should poison their relationship. And news like this would do. They preferred to bury the truth and let everyone believe that Germany was responsible for the crime.

Winds of Freedom Blow in Evros

The summer of '44 was hot for everyone in Europe. Developments on the Eastern Front and the triumphant Russian advance had demoralized the Germans. This was evident even in Evros.

At the time, there was a force of some 1500 Germans dispersed among the larger cities of Evros. The people were heartened by the successes of the Kellis team, unlike the Germans who were panic-stricken, as was also obvious by their behavior. It was as if they suddenly became courteous to the people. The moment was then ripe for the guerrillas to deliver a coup de grâce. Which is exactly what they did.

Rodney Young crossing Struma (Evros River) on ferry.

Only 600 rebels were armed and not with heavy weaponry. Though the initial thought was to begin with surprise attacks on German outposts in order to put more weapons into the hands of ELAS, the plan changed: at daybreak on August 29, the battles began at the transfer center for German forces in Evros in Didymoteichon. Lambros had the general command. The Germans were pounded from dawn until one o'clock in the afternoon of the following day. Defeated Germans tried to save themselves. Some reached the Evros river, where many drowned, while others managed to arrive at the border and cross to Turkey. The armaments they left behind proved a true treasure because they were modern and sufficient to equip all three thousand men of the 81st ELAS Regiment.

While the battle of Didymoteichon was ongoing, Athinodoros, a true son of Ferrai, entered the city at the head of a smaller force. He succeeded in doing so with cunning and intelligence that was analogous to that shown by Odysseus in the Cyclops myth. The result was by tricking the Germans he forced them to surrender without a shot being fired. That evening, four thousand residents from the surrounding villages assembled in the central square of the city, where they celebrated their liberation with songs and flags.

Next in line were the outposts of Peplos and Anthia and the garrison at Magazi. Soufli could easily have fallen too, had Lambros and Aris not lost the advantage of surprise by sending a committee to ask for their surrender.

The battle at Soufli started at dawn on August 31. It proved to be the most critical because the Germans not only attacked the rear of the guerrilla forces with their Aegean motorized unit at Alexandroupolis, but also had support by air. The situation was saved by the latest OSS armaments shipment, which arrived just at the right time. With these arms, Athinodoros set up the reserve of ELAS Ferrai with the objective of blocking the route to a force of a thousand Germans, expected to abandon Soufli and unite with the force of Alexandroupolis.

All in all, two hundred rebels from the hills around Magazi and Dadia literally crippled the motorized phalanx of Germans, at a distance of 60 kilometers from Anthia. At least twenty motorized vehicles were destroyed, which the Germans towed, along with their dead, to Alexandroupolis. In retaliation, however, small neighboring villages, connected by a central road, were burned down with flame-throwers. As a result, in less than a week — between August 28 and September 3 — Evros was liberated, with heavy losses for the Germans. The Greeks had only 8 dead and 12 injured, but many villages were destroyed. German deaths exceeded 150, more were injured and 410 were captured. But they lost large-scale heavy arms to Greek hands, as well as huge amounts of foodstuffs, automobiles, 28 trucks, motorcycles, bicycles and railroad material. The involvement of the people in those battles, even small children who distributed food and tobacco to the rebels, was moving. Their singing even obscured the sound of weapons and reached my ears as I observed the battles with binoculars from Turkey.

Evros became the first area on Greek soil to feel the sweet joy of freedom.

Georgiades along with another Greek-American officer crossing Macedonia after the liberation.

At Nea Vissa after the liberation.

The Bulgarian-Held Zone is Next

With the morale revived, the second and third divisions of the 81st ELAS battalion launched the operation to liberate Alexandroupolis from the Bulgarians on September 5.

It was preceded by the entrance to the city of the damaged mechanized unit of the Aegean with only 35 German vehicles remaining. The mood was so dismal that the populace and the Bulgarian soldiers were instructed to remain indoors, so as not to see the shabby condition of the Germans. The Bulgarian fascists were eagerly waiting to see the Germans returning as victors with the severed heads of guerrillas on stakes. But what they saw before them was entirely different.

Everyone was numb. At dawn, Athinodoros arrived in the city with two Bulgarian officers who had defected and formed a revolutionary committee. The committee's function was to enlighten the Bulgarian soldiers and persuade them to lay down their arms and surrender without resistance because things had changed and the Russian army was already in Sofia. The pro-fascist monarchist regime had fallen already and Bulgarian Communists had taken the situation in their hands. In vain, the fascist General Sirakoff, based in Drama, was trying to pass contrary instructions to the occupying army.

The Bulgarian settlers, meanwhile, were abandoning the houses they had settled in by displacing the locals. The Greeks in a burst of frenetic, joyous jubilation rushed out to the streets to pull down the signs from the streets and shops that were written in Bulgarian, to paint the walls and wipe out anything reminiscent of the Bulgarian occupation which, in terms of actions against the local populace, was even more brutal than that of the Germans.

When I learned that a major ELAS force led by Kritonas was about to depart for Alexandroupolis, I asked him to go along, too. I wanted to see things up close and first-hand. Given his noted distrust toward me, however, he refused under the pretext that he could not guarantee my safety. So I decided to disregard him and set off with Moravas.

The climate in the city was moving. People of all ages were in the streets and still celebrating and repairing whatever they found damaged by the occupying army. That was, of course, not true on the outskirts, where some fanatical fascist Bulgarians were burning whatever homes and facilities they found in their path.

It was impressive. I heard the guerrillas themselves remarking on how easily and swiftly the Bulgarian army had changed its flags, even the caps of their soldiers bore insignia with the red hammer and sickle. All of them spoke of the Allies in the fondest terms.

"Alas, the times…," I whispered to myself.

In mid-September, the Bulgarian occupation army officially left Alexandroupolis. I then decided to transfer my base there. No one in the rebel leadership liked this, of course, but I no longer cared. I had made it clear to them that, if they did not want me, they only needed to say so directly and honestly. Naturally, I told them also that I could not guarantee how this might be viewed in Cairo. They understood what I meant immediately.

Meanwhile, from Cyprus, a jeep arrived for my travels. Now I felt truly free to go anywhere I wanted. After all, that portion of Greece was liberated. Who could have prevented me from moving as I wished now, given that I had risked my life by entering Bulgarian-occupied territories for the needs of the Resistance?

Infiltrating Bulgaria

The Allied Office in Cairo attached great importance to intelligence collection from Bulgaria and Romania where the war was in the final phase.

On many occasions, I had to infiltrate both the occupied areas and Bulgarian territories to meet with clusters of the Bulgarian resistance, with whom our own guerrillas maintained contact.

At first, and more specifically from September 1943 onwards, I sent information I obtained from different travelers, students, merchants and refugees who I encountered along the Turkish-Bulgarian borders. Initially, I was able to obtain information with regard to Tsar Boris' hasty return from Germany, following incidents created in Sofia by students that resulted in the assassination of the monarch and certain deployments of military forces on Bulgarian soil, namely along the border on the side of Ortaköy, west of Alexandroupolis. During that period, I signed my dispatches with the code-name "Aster," which, for reasons I did not learn, Sperling had given me in Istanbul, which was code-named "Dover."

In October 1943, the Third Division of the Bulgarian Army moved and was deployed between Svilengrad and Malko Tarnavo. Colonel Iordanov had in the meantime arrived in Svilengrad from Lyubimets, in command of a sizable artillery unit, which was equipped with large quantities of ammunition that his men stored in voids east of the railway station, as well as in the elementary school of the town Kireşlik, between Svilengrad and Ortaköy. The Third Cavalry Regiment under the command of an officer called Yemitzieff was quartered at the town of Rakovski near Haskovo. The headquarters of the Cavalry and the Engineer Corps were at Philippopolis. Momchilgrad served as a refueling center; large fuel tanks and ammunition depots were located east of the city.

According to intelligence reported in the same month, the Bulgarians completed the construction of a camp, two miles to the east of Svilengrad, at the intersection of the highway leading to Istanbul. The camp had two quarters with clay tile roofs and several underground bunkers. Three AA guns provided a defense shield for both the town and the camp. The hills of Cherna Mogila, neighboring Svilengrad, were very well defended, according to various reports.

A line of defense was established along a vast area from the Black Sea to Svilengrad, due to the deployment of a powerful cavalry force. The entire Second Brigade, consisting of six battalions and one mechanized infantry battalion, was positioned along the defense line of the Turkish-Bulgarian borders, obviously because of apprehensions that Turkey might abandon its neutrality.

Drawing on a highly credible source, I informed Cairo that Bulgarians had planted mines from the Ainos Mountain to Samothrace, including the port of Alexandroupolis.

One could see there was also extensive activity on the neighboring island of Lesvos. The captain of a caique confided to me that a German force of 300 men and 30 combat aircraft were stationed at the island's airfield.

On the same day, I learned that three Italian destroyers with Italian and German crews were berthed in Alexandroupolis. Bulgarians were camped at Aisymi, Sapes and Komotini, under the command of Colonels Milief and Zlatanoff, respectively.

The preparation of the Axis air force was much more extensive. In February 1944, I informed Cairo of the fortification works carried out at the Malevo airfield. The Germans were building an airstrip that was over three kilometers long and were also able to employ the auxiliary airfields Bulgaria had used until then. They also constructed depots and fuel tanks into which 20 large tanker trucks unloaded gasoline. All buildings had camouflaged roofs. Malevo was also the base for 80-100 combat aircraft, some single-engine, others with twin- or even three-engines.

During February, the Germans requisitioned also the Yambol airfield, which was five kilometers long and two kilometers wide, along with numerous underground depots where 300 gasoline tanks were kept. At this airfield, 150 German combat aircraft and only 10-15 Bulgarian single-engine aircraft were positioned. We received a significant piece of intelligence, sourced to the German High Command, which reported that all soldiers under 40 years old would be replaced by older personnel. The first replacement took place at the town of Elhovo.

I entered Bulgarian territory via Turkey twice because the agreement between Athinodoros' guerrillas and Kellis signed at the Lefkimi hideout — which I sent from Adrianople to Cairo before the "Chicago" operation began — stipulated that the guerrillas, who in any event were in contact with the Bulgarian partisans long before we arrived at Evros, would pass to us the information the latter gave them. According to the agreement, each guerrilla would be given one golden pound each month for the duration of the operation.

After the completion of the operation, during which Evros was liberated, immense confusion prevailed during the time that elapsed between the withdrawal of the Bulgarians from the Bulgarian-occupied Greek territory and the march of the Russian Army into Sofia, which occurred with about two weeks of delay. It was during that time that Major James Bruce and two more men arrived at Didymoteichon en route from Cairo in order to enter Bulgaria and evaluate the situation. The guerrillas helped these three men reach out to Yemitzieff, commander of a force of Bulgarian partisans, who happened to have participated in the battle at Soufli. Yemitzieff agreed to liaise Bruce with guerrillas who waited to take him to Sofia. He also helped him board a train to Svilengrad. From there, others would take over. Yemitzieff stayed behind to participate in mopping-up operations against pockets of Bulgarians aligned with fascist General Sirakoff, who held their positions, and allied themselves with combatants of Tsaus Anton and the British under the command of the notorious Miller to strike EAM-ELAS.

Speculation that emerged from this cooperation turned against Bruce, who supposedly asked Yemitzieff to speak before a public rally in the main square of Soufli, recognizing in this way that Bulgarians had a role to play in the region, is completely false. The truth of the matter is that Bruce, a very low profile officer, barely agreed to speak to me for less than five-minute address in the main square of Didymoteichon before an enormously enthusiastic crowd. In Soufli, where Yemitzieff delivered his own speech, the people were in such a frenzy that they did not care who the speaker would be as long as he could share their happiness. It was none of Bruce's business whatsoever whether the Bulgarian military gave a speech. After all, how could an officer of the US Army ask an officer of another country to address the people of a country which was foreign to both?

Captain Bruce disguised in a German uniform.

The First Weeks of Freedom

Only the lens of an accomplished cinema director could capture the frantic joy and enthusiasm the day after the departure of the dual occupation troops from this neglected corner of the country. Evros had been among the poorest prefectures even before the war and its populace had endured an abundance of punishing hardships. Most of the people who lived there were illiterate, tillers of the soil and stockbreeders, craftsmen and day-laborers. One day, they saw their property, accumulated through lifetimes of struggle, destroyed by retaliations, larceny and confiscation.

The Germans, who had occupied the area bordering on Turkey, not only plundered the annual crop from the barns, but also stole the few eggs meticulously put aside by mothers to feed their young children. I recall that story because of something that still torments me.

I was impressed by the fact that people living in the villages I went to complained about Germans who burst in their houses hoping to find eggs to send to Germany for their own families. After listening to their complaints, I thought I would take revenge on the Germans. I thought of getting hold of a syringe in order to pierce the eggs they seized and inject them with arsenic. When I visited Sperling in Istanbul one day, I asked him to provide me with a small quantity of this poison. He asked me what I would do with it. When Virginia Grace, who was present in that meeting, heard what I was planning to do, she was horrified. She turned to me and said: "Dear Lord, Alex! Are you insane? Do you plan to kill little children in Germany to wreak your revenge on their fathers?" I was dazed and dumbstruck. In my raging desire to take revenge on the Germans for all the evils they had caused to those helpless people, I had begun to resemble them...

When I met with Virginia in Athens in 1965, where she was an archaeologist at the American School of Classical Studies, I reminded her of that incident and thanked her for preventing me from committing an evil I would regret for the rest of my life. Sitting side-by-side in the garden across the Gennadius School, we discussed how war could transform people, unbeknownst to them, into beasts.

Virginia Grace, an archaeologist from New York, excavated in Pergamon
and in Cyprus. She worked for OSS and was assigned to the Çeşme base.
She died in 1994 in Athens, where she had lived the remainder of her life,
working as a member of the American Archaeological School.

After the liberation, ELAS guerrillas came down from the
mountains and undertook to guard Alexandroupolis, the largest regional
city. Moravas was appointed garrison commander and EAM took over
the political administration. I remained in the region for about two weeks,
traveling between Alexandroupolis and Komotini, making brief stopovers
in various towns and villages for a first-hand look on developments.

I remember the first problem that ELAS needed to resolve with
the Bulgarians was settling the issue of the fish cannery facility that their
occupation authorities built in Alexandroupolis. This had to be done
without orders from Sofia, since the situation there was still uncertain
because the pro-Hitler government of Bogdan Filof was collapsing and
the Greek-Bulgarian conflict over the cannery's ownership was inevitably
being transferred to Greek hands. Through its representative, Lambros
Kanakaris, ELAS managed to broker an agreement with Kioumoutzieff,
the commanding officer of the Bulgarian partisans, according to which
all facilities and equipment would remain in Greece and commodities
would be shared equally and fairly.

A few days later, and after fresh fighting between Bulgarian rebels and Germans retreating east of the Struma River, the new government in Sofia officially announced it would relinquish Bulgarian-occupied Greek territory to Greece — unfortunately, however, not without bloodshed. As hard-line enclaves of the Bulgarian army still remained in the region, civilians who had been brought in to colonize and Slavicise the Greek territories reacted and unleashed a vengeful armed campaign against the Greek population, which had already suffered incredible brutality and humiliation from the notorious Ohrana (Protection), the Bulgaria secret services.

From Alexandroupolis, I decided to move further east because I learned that ELAS forces, including Kritonas and Aris, were moving in that direction to support ELAS guerrillas who were under attack by fighters who supported Tsaus Anton and were backed by the British and the infamous Miller. But the ELAS leadership were not happy. For some reason, they resented my presence amongst them.

But I did not back down. I reacted in turn by telling Lambros to stop telling me what I should and should not do; otherwise, I threatened, he would leave me no choice but to leave. This, I knew was something they did not want since they still needed me. The situation was unstable and everything was in a state of flux. So, he had no choice but to give me a letter asking ELAS to provide me whatever I needed to enable me to go wherever I wanted to.

The jeep, which arrived at the ideal time, allowed me more freedom of movement and so I went to Komotini. This town had the biggest agricultural production in all of Thrace and was of special interest due to the Muslim population which lived between there and the adjacent town of Drama, where the Turkish Consulate was located.

Upon arrival, I found the locals extremely worried because of rumors that the Russians were about to descend on their area. Memories of Bulgarian atrocities remained vivid among the people, who harbored a profound and justified resentment against Slavs for what they had done to them during the German occupation. The mere thought that Russians could rush to help Bulgarians, who would thus seize on a second opportunity for a much-coveted exit to the Aegean, filled them with horror and dread.

Here, I must emphasize that the communists had identical fears. Indeed, there was no one across the entire political spectrum, between the two extremes, who did not have similar fears. Perhaps the best indication came from the Muslim population. They had suffered the least oppression due to protection they had from the local consulate and Turkey's declared neutrality. Using my Turkish language skills, I roamed among their villages to better understand how they felt at such prospects. And, of course, my surprise was more than pleasant. The people spoke in the worst way possible of the Bulgarians and prayed that no such evils would befall them again.

After I had gained their trust — since they were unaware I was half Greek and saw me only as an American who had come to help them —, they spoke openly and without fear to me. They told me how pleased they were with their lives in Greece, that they got along well with Greeks and had friendly relations with many of them, that they had their own schools and mosques and, in short, they never wanted to return to Turkey. Proof of which was their burgeoning numbers, which during the war years had reached about eighty-thousand people. I admit to being stunned because I had not known their exact number. Subconsciously, however, I compared them to Greeks in Turkey. There, the Turkish regime invented ways to persecute them on a daily basis, to drive them out of their homes, forcing them to abandon their property in the very homeland where they were born, or confiscating it and then sending them to execution sites or labor camps, like Erzurum, famed for Capital Tax (*Varlık Vergisi*).

In Komotini, I met a remarkable man, Costas Konstandaras, an officer of the Greek Army, when he and Aris came to see me. Aris' real name was Mikhalis Sougioglou. He was unrelated to the other Aris Daskalaris, who was assassinated by the Germans and was succeeded by Odysseus who became infamous for his atrocities. Guerrillas had a penchant for the name Aris and used it extensively. Aris was the name of the God of War in ancient Greece.

Konstandaras was recruited by ELAS and was useful to them as their officer because he knew about war. He was not a communist and the ELAS guerrillas were aware of that. Our discussions were extremely helpful because I was able to understand much of what led to the civil war.

I joined him in duck hunting and his wife cooked the game for all three of us on the following day. He seemed to be a trustworthy fellow: honest and with pellucid reasoning. Aris was much like him. But Aris was a communist and necessarily followed the official party line. Konstandaras' thinking was infinitely more valuable to me.

While chatting with him and Aris, I realized that both disagreed with Article 5 of the Lebanon Agreement. This stipulated that the restoration of law and order after the war in Greece would be carried out with the assistance of the allied powers. They could see no reason why foreigners should be involved in a country that paid such a high price for its independence. They had strong suspicions, which were vindicated, that the British sowed discord in Greece and led the Greeks to civil war, bent as they were upon restoring the monarchy in Greece.

Konstandaras was even more furious with the Caserta Agreement. He, as a military officer, could not accept the Greek Armed Forces being subjected to British command and the transformation of Greece into a British colony!

"Do you understand, Alekos, what is at stake here? It's inconceivable! We have so many competent and efficient generals serving our national armed forces. How can they abolish us with a sheet of paper and the stroke of a pen?"

He stared at me, red-faced with anger. As I am writing this, I recollect a report drafted by my friend Costas Couvaras, a journalist from New York, also recruited by the OSS. I will write about him more extensively below because Costas was a stalwart and fought hard to make his views known. He even appeared before the Senate on March 31, 1947, to testify about his activities in Greece.

Costas wrote a book published by Exantas Publications titled "OSS with the Central Committee of EAM." In it he writes the following about Plastiras, as was narrated to him by a close friend and associate of the former Prime Minister, on April 2, 1945: "The British are playing a dirty game in Greece and Plastiras is, in essence, their prisoner. They put him in an awkward position right from the very beginning, when he had no idea what the game was. When the British brought him to Greece from abroad, they asked him to make intransigent remarks and now they are asking him to be conciliatory. At the same time, the British secret services are operating in diametrically opposed ends, by using their surrogates to discredit him, which makes him extremely upset because he can understand what in fact is going on. A few days ago, he discovered that the Ministry of Military Affairs is powerless and that genuine power lies in the hands of two pro-royalist colonels, whose machinations cannot be countervailed by his minister, a man in whom Plastiras has utter confidence." The Prime Minister's friend concluded by saying the British can cast aside Plastiras easily anytime they please.

Regardless of what we learned later, we could clearly see the role of the wily Major Miller, whose real name was Guy Micklethwait, commander of the British forces in Eastern Macedonia as of January 1943. He operated in the Paggaio mountains and provided supplies both to the guerrillas of ELAS and the unit of Tsaus Anton, who collaborated with the Bulgarian fascists of General Sirakoff to conduct strikes against ELAS. The British achieved two goals at once: they controlled the influence EAM-ELAS exerted in Greece and also the developments in adjacent Bulgaria, where the enclaves of fascism had not been yet eradicated.

The most excessive and cowardly act of the British was the execution of eighteen ELAS guerrillas on New Year's Eve of 1944 by pro-Tsaus Anton fighters, while they were all celebrating the arrival of the new year. Ten more ELAS guerrillas were then executed at the Zarnovitsa village after they had received British equipment dropped in the mountains of Drama, as a result of Miller's duplicity. Following this dual crime, the notorious Miller relinquished his insidious title and openly sided with Tsaus Anton. What a tragedy. Regrettably, this has been Greece's record for ages. An abiding requiem of glory and defeat, of gallantry and treachery.

Konstandaras, was a genuine patriot and honorable officer, as were so many Greeks who fought against the invader, only to be forgotten later and relegated to the fringes of history. Konstandaras was not only imprisoned and his rank rescinded, never to be restored until his death at the age of 65 from heart disease; he also lived impoverished, deriving his sole income from tutoring fees. He was among the friends I met in 1965, during my only visit to Greece after the war. I remember I found him in a genuinely wretched state of poverty which he tried to veil with humor and, foremost, with the dignity that distinguished him throughout his life.

There were many patriots who fought on the side of ELAS against the occupiers, but who were not necessarily communists. Couvaras offers a nice account of this in his book when he describes the conversation he had with a farmer's boy, George, whom the guerrillas assigned to him as an escort when his delegation arrived at Euboea from Smyrna:

"Why did you join the guerrillas, George, since you are not a communist?" he asked him.

"I became a guerrilla to fight the enemies of my country," George answered. He did not have the faintest idea about Marxist ideology and he had never thought that he would have to live the life he led in the mountains. He merely heeded the call of patriotic duty to go out and fight against the enemy. That's what he did, that was his "crime."

During that period, while I traipsed from town to city and from village to hamlet, the first delegates of the Greek command of Macedonia arrived, first in Serres, then in Kavala and later in Drama and Komotini. Until that time, EAM and ELAS had the interim responsibility of command.

As I wore civilian clothes and did not arouse suspicions, I was able to join the group of officials and observe at close quarters the touching manner in which ordinary people welcomed them with cheers of joy and enthusiasm. It was especially moving to see young children stop in the middle of the street, gather stones and put them in their bags or in carts for use later in rebuilding their demolished houses, while also waving at the government officials. Among the latter was Colonel Prokos, escorted by the chief of the British military force for Northern Greece, Major General Kay Boick, the new provincial governor Kostopoulos, Lampriniadis, Porfyrogenis and several lower-ranking officers of the army.

Generally, there was an atmosphere of protracted joy and optimism that prevented anyone from noticing the approaching storm. Seeing German hostages forced by the locals to work hard in order to rebuild what they had destroyed and the sight of Bulgarian soldiers with red scarves tied around their necks marching and singing as they left was more than enough to make your spirits soar.

A few days later, I went to Soufli. There, I met Young who in the meantime had been relieved of his duties from the Greek Office in Cairo and worked for UNRRA. I took him by jeep to Alexandroupolis. Shortly before reaching the city, at the Korneofolia site, people stopped us when they saw the American flag on the jeep. They asked us to help a poor pilot, who had made a forced landing nearby and kept repeating the only word they could understand, "American, American." They held him in confinement because swastikas were painted on the aircraft. When we saw them, we explained to them that our pilots were accustomed to painting a swastika for each German aircraft they shot down and it was obvious that the pilot they had arrested had shot down several enemy aircraft.

We asked them to take us to him. As soon as he saw us, he was relieved and saluted us, although we were both in civilian clothes. We took him with us to Alexandroupolis. I contacted the OSS headquarters in Caserta, where the Command had been relocated from Cairo, to tell them about the pilot, so that Caserta could inform the pilot's air base. I asked for further instructions regarding the fate of the aircraft. Kritonas, who was pursuing Tsaus Anton fighters on the outskirts of the city, had in the meantime removed its machine gun. Young took the pilot to Thessaloniki, and I left for Xanthi with the wireless technicians.

Kritonas was after Tsaus Anton and his close to three thousand supporters, armed by the British. They were scattered, but still dangerous. This was clear in documents ELAS obtained, which detailed how Tsaus Anton, Miller and Sirakoff planned to combine their forces in order to incapacitate ELAS and cross into Bulgaria with the aim of reaching Sofia.

Their plans failed, however, because ELAS printed and signed the documents in both Greek and Bulgarian, so that Greek and Bulgarians partisans would take the necessary precautions. I am writing these things for people to learn that not only communists, who after all fought against the Germans, but also fascists collaborated with the Bulgarians. The same fascists who butchered Greeks and looted their property during the Bulgarian occupation.

Let me note briefly here something Couvaras writes about the press in Greece that even in the tough war years sought to sway public opinion. Besides people like me and a dozen Americans who witnessed it first-hand, who would have thought that people read daily and weekly newspapers and magazines in the mountain areas? It was in print that I saw Dimitrios Partsalides' photograph and could not believe my eyes. Where printed material could not be delivered, we used megaphones. In Karpathos, we had the town crier with kids running behind him, but in the mountains we had EAM fighters who climbed onto the highest point of the town and used the megaphone to announce the news to the public:

"Yesterday, Hitler's men suffered their worst defeat in the war in Stalingrad. American aircraft bombarded German targets with stunning success..." Yes, this is how Greeks are. They are the same whenever and wherever they have to fight in combat, no matter if they have nothing to eat or coffee to drink at the coffee houses of their villages or at a cafe or are immigrants in New York.

In any event, after Miller was exposed, he vanished from the face of the earth. He did not dare to be seen in public. The British must have relocated him in the night. I cannot recall who replaced him or what his name was. I only remember that his nickname was "Kit Kat" and that his assistant was called MacDonald. Kit Kat had four sergeants working with him, all of whom were probably wireless operators.

Alex at downed P-51 outside the city of Alexandroupolis.

Greek children excited on downed P-51.

Every Era Has Its Ephialtes[1]

The land of my ancestors, thousands of miles from the land where I now write these lines, has been not only the birthplace of heroes but also of despicable traitors. One might think God permitted their kind to be brought forth, so that the genuine heroes of that small country, with the greatest history on earth, would be praised more highly. Ephialtes, who once betrayed Leonidas to the Persians at Thermopylae, had a different name in my era. The name of the traitor who received his 30 pieces of silver, or rather, gold pounds, from the barbarous royalist-fascists was Tsaus Anton, whose real name was Fosteridis.

Fosteridis always managed to slip away whenever his foul, criminal role was unveiled. This was not only because of luck, but more thanks to persons of his ilk who have proved useful to anti-democratic regimes throughout the course of history.

When he was arrested, accused of collaborating with the anti-Hellène Sirakoff, and taken in custody to Athens supposedly to be tried for treason, the whole operation proved nothing but a fiasco. By necessity, he was allowed to be taken elsewhere to avoid execution by ELAS, which had already executed about 300 collaborators of the Bulgarians.

As I do not wish to be accused of antipathy or bias against him, I will let historians refute me when the history of the Greek Civil War is rewritten. Was he or was he not released during the "Dekemvriana" events in order to butcher people again? Moreover, is it not a coincidence that his family, who continued to live in Thrace even after the war, was one of the wealthiest in the region?

What worked greatly to his advantage was the immense confusion not only at the highest levels of the fledgling government, but also among the people. Wherever one happened to be in those days, everyone, both rightists and leftists, complained incessantly and of course criticized the Lebanon and Caserta decisions. Ordinary people were perhaps the only ones entitled to complain. Their leaders, though aware of Churchill's intransigent stance and his sole concern for the return of the abhorrent Glücksburg dynasty at any cost, signed all agreements even after Papandreou's had called them brigands and murderers.

---

[1] An ancient Athenian politician and an early leader of the democratic movement there.

In that atmosphere, it would make sense for someone to give up hope on the possibility of progress or a proper, let alone fair, decision.

On September 10, 1944, the radio stations of London and Moscow urged ELAS to halt attacks on Bulgarian troops left behind within Greek territory because on the previous day Bulgaria had surrendered unconditionally to Russian Field Marshal Fyodor Tolbukhin whose army had invaded their country and made its forces available to the Allies.

In fact, by the end of October, all Bulgarians had returned to their homeland. While one might have expected that winds of optimism of the initial days would continue to blow — when everyone, regardless of faction, rejoiced in unison —, the first pro-royalists demonstrations began, asking for the return of the king.

Those demonstrations, of course, were neither widespread nor extensive. The demonstrators were school children carrying identity cards supplied to them by the Intelligence Service, obviously with some minor remuneration as well. They came out into the streets with rallying cries for a greater Greece ruled by the King, yet they were unable to defend their words or explain why they and their fathers had not taken up arms against the occupiers as other young people of their age had done. Their demonstrations stirred up reactions by EPON, which scattered them whenever it intervened against them.

This is how developments unfolded, first in cities, beginning with persecution of EAM-ELAS collaborators, followed by armed conflict, during which precious Greek blood would be shed depriving the country of the flower of its youth.

On only a few occasions was this not necessary, for instance in Xanthi. There, Kritonas, who was persecuting Tsaus Anton fighters, managed to convince them to unite and to bring them back with him after they promised him they would not strike against ELAS again. He also disarmed them. If only others had acted like him, the country would have been spared the bloodshed.

I continued my trip to Kavala. I wanted to see how things were going, knowing I would meet Aris and Konstandaras there. As soon as I arrived in the city, they took me to the mayor's house. His name was Vassilikos. As I learned later, he was the uncle of Vassilis Vassilikos, author of "Z." He was a really interesting man who enjoyed a good reputation as a doctor in the local society. I met him again a few times, including one time when he was at a restaurant in Kavala with ELAS officers.

Then, an incident occurred, which I remember quite well. It provided the occasion to become acquainted with another EAM member, who impressed me with his knowledge, sangfroid and moderation — virtues which, if more possessed them, matters would have taken a different turn.

As usual, the primary subject of our discussion was the political situation. We had been having that discussion for a while, when someone else at the table spoke so loudly that his words were heard by all:

"Isn't it striking that a person such as the American in our company has such progressive views, although he is not a communist?"

Perplexed, I turned and looked at him.

"Let me tell you something, young man. Marxism may be good in theory, but what about human rights and liberties? And since you are asking me in front of everyone else here, let me tell you that I would never relinquish the civil liberties the American Constitution offers me for the sake of the proletariat."

An awkward silence fell among us for a few seconds, broken by the voice of someone whose presence I had not noticed until then:

"Alekos is right!"

I was surprised he knew my name because I had never met him before. He continued, however, looking in my direction.

"Listen, Alekos, we know who you are and why your government sent you here. We also know why you were given orders to cooperate with us. It's not because they're sympathetic toward us or became communists themselves. It's because they realized that without us the Germans and Bulgarians would have never left Greece under any circumstances. Regarding your Constitution, I can only say this: If you Americans manage to implement all the articles of the Jeffersonian Constitution in their entirety, then, let it be understood, communism will ipso facto lose meaning and cease to exist. The issue is whether you will ever do it. I very much doubt it… In any case, it's not the politicians but the multinationals that govern your country. If in the future a government is installed in Greece which will not serve their interests, then Americans will do to Greece the same things the British are doing today — and if that occurs, I am very much afraid that you will be in trouble with your peers back in America, regardless of whether you follow their orders today."

I invited him to come to sit at our table. It seemed to me he was a clever interlocutor, but also composed and without ideological fixations. We spoke for hours on historical subjects, too. He was a well-read individual.

Because he left the restaurant first, I was able to ask, "Does anyone know his name?"

They all looked at one another in amazement.

"You were talking with him for so long, Alekos, and you did not realize with whom you were dealing? He is the Communist Party Secretary, Petros."

They did not tell me his surname, though I found out later that he was killed in the second round of the civil war.

As days went by, hunger and misery reigned. Blood was unjustifiably and unreasonably spilled. I knew many people whose abilities and ingenuity were wasted. With so many things happening, my uncertainty increased even about the kind of information I filed back to my country. I was not sure whatever I saw and heard made any sense. What bewildered me more, however, was that no one seemed interested in what was going on in Greece, this forgotten corner of the world in which the young, as was made clear, had no future.

Even in those days, it was evident to me that young people were prepared to leave the country. This is not something easily grasped by those who have not experienced the suffering of living abroad. I experienced this sort of suffering about 60 years ago. And yet a piece of my heart stayed behind, in the village I was born in…

From Evros to Thessaloniki and then Athens:
The Civil War Breaks Out

It was in early October that I received an order to depart for Thessaloniki in order to meet with Sperling.

Frangoulis and Tsiaparas traveled with me. I drove in my jeep all the way up to Thessaloniki and all I could see were ruins. The road was thick with huge potholes that needed to be cautiously avoided if we were to arrive on time. Frangoulis and Tsiaparas did not stop for a moment making remarks on what we saw and asking me for stopovers, so that they could photograph things. We seldom encountered people. Now and then, we saw a few men and women, shadows of themselves, in fact, walking skeletons, like ghosts, emaciated by hunger and deprivations. They appeared out of nowhere upon hearing the sound of the jeep and then instantly faded from view.

Alex upon his arrival at Thessaloniki after the liberation.

In Thessaloniki, we were put up in a very beautiful two-story house at Panorama area across from the building that today houses the

American Agricultural School. From my window, I could see the sea shimmering under the autumn sun. A light breeze caressed its surface, as if to intimate that Vardaris, the fierce northern wind, was on its way…

The view of Mount Olympos. Georgiades shot the picture
from his room in Panorama (Thessaloniki).

Even more majestic was the sight of Olympus. I could clearly see that the peak was already snow-capped. Three thousand years of the mythology and history of a great people were condensed in this iconic symbol: Olympus.

New orders arrived that sent me to meet Markos Vafiadis and General Bakirtzis instead of Sperling. As long as the British continued their dirty games, which created additional danger every day, it was essential for us to know how ELAS would react in Macedonia, where it maintained a significant force. Obviously, since I served for an extended period in that region, I was the only one the ELAS guerrillas knew and trusted. This is why I was given the order.

In the meantime, though still standing, there were signs that physical and mental fatigue were setting in. The general rule was that OSS men ought not to be fielded for more than six months, whereas I broke every record by being deployed to Greece for an entire year and a half. Every day, I awaited the order calling me back. So, when I received an order to go to Athens, I believed the countdown had begun. But I was wrong. I will explain below why and how matters transpired.

Upon my arrival in Athens, I went to the OSS office, if I remember correctly on 1 Feidiou Street, a side street of Panepistimiou Avenue. The chief of mission was a Wisconsin University professor named Gerald Else. His deputy assistant was a man called Freer and Pauline Manos was his secretary. I was acquainted with her from the Greek Office in Cairo, where she served in the same capacity.

I asked for a short furlough in order to visit my relatives, who I had not seen in years. They lived in Piraeus, where they had settled after leaving Karpathos. My sister, who was married and had her own family, also lived there. I was anxious to meet them and get to know my nieces and nephews. I was delighted when Else gave me a few days' off, so I could stay with them. Soon, their house resembled more a transit center as friends, relatives and neighbors paid daily visits to greet and meet "the American" and learn something as the situation was deteriorating alarmingly with each passing day. Rumors were rife and people were bitterly disappointed with the government and with Papandreou personally, who had been received with so much enthusiasm a month earlier. Those who were once regarded as heroic fighters because they fought against the Germans in the mountains and in the cities were now met with hostility. The security battalions and collaborators of the Germans, on the other hand, continued to be armed by the British and Scobie, who, after Lebanon, had been given general command of the military in order to persecute the former.

Georgiades reunion with his sister's family living in Piraeus.

Numerous stories have been told over time, but having lived through the events, first in Northern Greece and then in Athens, I can attest to this: If ELAS wanted to seize power through force, as it was accused of intending to do, it could have refused to sign the Agreements of Lebanon and Caserta, simply because, if it had such an intention, it could have done this much earlier and ignored Cairo and the Allies. The only resistance to their plans would probably have been EDES in Epirus, but even so, ELAS could comfortably neutralize it as it did when armed conflict erupted with Zervas, Tsaus Anton and Michalangas in Epirus, Thrace and Macedonia, respectively. I understood why the leaders of ELAS in Northern Greece had expressed dissatisfaction at those two notorious Agreements.

I must admit that all of us, the Americans who staffed the UNRRA, the Greek War Relief Office of the OSS and the airmen at the Eleufsis Air Base, shared the feelings of the Greek people. I want to be clear about this because I do not want anyone to think I am here expressing personal views about the disputes within the Government of National Unity in November 1945, concerning the composition of the National Army, which led to the bloodshed of the Civil War. ELAS' proposal that the structure of the new National Armed Forces, under joint command, had to consist of one EDES battalion, one army battalion from the Middle East and two battalions of ELAS were rejected by Papandreou and the British.

The fuse was lit in early December when a British plane flew over Athens and Piraeus and dropped leaflets announcing that Scobie and British troops would remain in the country to protect the people and the Greek Government against anyone threatening to seize power by use of arms. ELAS was not specifically mentioned, but it was not difficult for anyone to understand who they meant.

EAM and ELAS responded immediately and called upon the Greek people to hold a massive demonstration on December 3, for which the police initially granted permission and then revoked. At the OSS offices, we were all on alert. MacVeagh asked Else to rescind my furlough and send Costas Couvaras and myself out to the streets to observe what was going on. I recalled immediately that some Karpathians I knew lived in Nea Smyrni and so I went to see them to learn how things were going.

Meanwhile, people began to gather in Constitution Square holding Greek, American and Russian flags. British flags were not seen anywhere.

Suddenly, from adjacent terraces, the Palace, the Papandreou residence, and from the office of the military commander Katsotas, shots were fired and people stopped singing songs of the Resistance. More than 20 young boys and girls were killed on that day and a much larger number of injured demonstrators fell to the ground. Instantly, the initial silence and stupefaction of the demonstrators changed into rage and people began anew to shout the slogans for unity and against the British. This shameful aspect of their history is known only to a few in England, not even among those who love ancient Greek classicism, precisely because an official historiography is lacking.

Following the tragic turn of events, EAM's representatives in the government resigned and a general strike occurred. Civil War broke out on the day after the funeral of the victims. There were 500,000 Athenians in the procession to the cemetery, all lamenting and mourning, reminiscent of a massive Greek chorus. Destiny, also in this case, as described in the dramatic conventions of Greek tragedies, appeared impossible to escape — which once again confirmed that the character of Greek history is an endless requiem of glory, defeat and mistakes.

The excuse for the outbreak of hostilities was Scobie's ultimatum saying that, unless the ELAS forces evacuated Athens and Piraeus by December 6, they would be executed at gunpoint. No Americans, including me, who were in Athens could ever comprehend or justify this unacceptable decision by the British. They threatened to execute people with whom they had fought against the enemy side by side, in their own country. No one could ever imagine that the people who struggled to see their country liberated would be so unfairly and brutally treated.

I lived through all these developments, I saw them with my very own eyes, which is why until I die I am not going to change my mind and I will tell everyone I encounter that EAM and ELAS are not to blame for the Civil War. The blame is on Churchill, Papandreou and their minions, that is, Woodhouse, their Ambassador Leaper and all the Intelligence Service operatives. These played a duplicitous game against the Greek people, their sole objective being the restoration of the King, whom President Roosevelt dubbed "empty-headed" when they met in Washington in 1942. He found him deficient and vacuous.

ELAS rejected Scobie's ultimatum immediately and hostilities erupted. Although ELAS possessed smaller forces and its equipment was vastly more inferior, its position was more advantageous in that it had the general command in Athens and Piraeus, whereas the British held only one enclave in Athens and one in Piraeus, the Hellenic Naval Academy.

It would have been impossible for me to believe what I saw then, or even imagine it, had I not seen it with my own eyes.

"Costa, I went mad. Do you know who I saw well-attired and gussied up with British uniforms? Mr. so-and-so."

Couvaras listened to me in amazement as I named the specific security battalion members and Grivas' "Chites," who, instead of being in prison, strutted around in brand-new British military uniforms, ready to kill again after a long time, if necessary.

"Well, what do you know?" Couvaras remarked. "If I tell you I'm unimpressed, what will you say?" Being a genuine New York journalist, he did not have my provincial naiveté.

"Chites" (members of the anticommunist and pro-royalist "Organization X"), security battalion members and police officers, organized by Papandreou upon his return to Athens, along with the Rimini Brigade, fought against ELAS guerrillas. But there was one difference: the latter had received orders, following a ridiculous notice, from the then deputy chief of ELAS Athens George Siantos, not to return fire because the uniforms did not allow them to distinguish between Greeks and British — and Siantos did not want Greeks among the victims.

I turned around and told him, "I am not the only clueless person in this town, Costas." He finally seemed surprised.

This, I assumed, was the reason why they earmarked only the ELAS reserve forces for battle. And yet, when someone took the initiative to order a detachment of about 700 fighters from the Ano Liossa battalion to come down to Athens as reinforcements, the initiative fell through because somewhere between Marathon and Aghia Paraskevi the detachment was confronted by a British armored infantry division and disarmed. When a decision was made to send new reinforcements, I asked permission from Erle to go to Liossa and find out if the information was valid.

I went to Liossa through Eleufsis for security reasons and there I saw about three thousand men on alert, restless and seeking the latest news from me. As did their leader, named Orestis, who was a teacher from Euboea. His real surname was Moundrinas and he knew many things about me and my action in Macedonia, proof that their internal communications system functioned flawlessly.

"You should have been there to see the great welcome they gave me," I told Couvaras. "As soon as I stepped out of the jeep, the military band played and sang paeans for me. A general would have been envious of such honors!"

We broke into laughter. Little did I know that, unbeknownst to me, someone was taking photos of me from behind and flanking me, making it clear I was at an ELAS camp. Jim Charakas from the OSS Chicago gave me those photographs many years later.

"How did he find them?"

I also had misgivings then about the issue of the revolver he asked from me when we returned to America. I had mailed it by pouch as a token and, as he said, he wanted to give it as a gift to the son of a US Secretary. It suddenly occurred to me that there was something suspicious about him.

Since I traveled back and forth to Liossa many times during that period, I came to know Orestis quite well. Else once asked a US Navy officer from Philadelphia to accompany me as an escort. Nichols was his name and he too worked for the OSS.

I return to Orestis below.

Back to Macedonia

Coming back from Liossa, around December 10, Else asked to meet me in his office, where he gave me new orders to go to the town of Florina. He wanted me to replace our liaison in Western Macedonia, John Franklin Daniel — aka "Duck" or "Pete" — for a short period as he had fallen sick. He was an archaeologist, too, and had worked in Cyprus before the war because he spoke Greek rather well. He was at our base in Kastellorizo before coming to Macedonia.

As soon as I received the order, I left Else's office to prepare without delay. I had to pack all my belongings because I did not know if I would be returning to my sister's house again. She was naturally worried by my unexpected departure, since she thought I would stay with her longer before returning to America. I thought the same, of course, but who could be confident under the circumstances? I did my best to ease her concerns without telling her exactly where I was going. My mission had to remain unknown.

My uttermost concern was to safely stash away all documents and notes I had brought back from Evros. Our standing directives were to never keep, for any reason, the written orders we were given concerning our contacts and operations. Since I knew I had violated them, I asked my nephew to destroy them if he thought there was a risk of the papers falling into the hands of someone else. As it turned out, this discerning young man — who shared this secret with me as well as the location in the house where I had hidden my documents — acted lightning fast during house-to-house searches in Piraeus for possible hiding places of ELAS weapons.

The Indian corps from the 5th Brigade included many hard-boiled Nepalese Gurkhas, notorious for their ferocity, for which they were recruited by the British arrived in our neighborhood and began knocking on doors of houses to search. My nephew disposed of the papers. He told me he burned them. But he did not manage to burn some papers given to me by Aris and Kritonas. Those as well as a stiletto, a German helmet, and my .45 pistol, which of course I had previously unloaded, were found and taken. Unfortunately, I was unable to locate these items when I returned.

I left Athens early in the afternoon and expected to arrive at the town of Livadia before nightfall. The roads were in a miserable state and full of potholes. There was wrecked military equipment discarded in heaps on both sides of the road and the roadway narrowed dangerously in several places. Yet, my jeep remained steadfast. It turned out to be quite a beast.

Unlike me, I must say, for at that very instant I felt crushed for the first time. Until then, thoughts never passed my mind even once that something bad could happen to me, that I might be killed. I had not felt the slightest fear while roaming from one side of Athens to another amid British and ELAS gunfire, yet suddenly a very intense agony seized me, something like panic broke out when, while driving, my gaze fell on the bullet-riddled windshield. I pulled to a stop at the side of the road and burst into tears. My body shook. I realized I needed to rest. That I could not go on.

I felt the same symptoms when I returned from the north after the end of the first round of the Civil War and did not want to go into Athens despite the fact that the fighting had stopped. I remember that, during the first night after my return, I went to the American Air Base at Eleufsis to sleep in order to recover.

Even today, at this age, those very same symptoms have not yet abandoned me. Unfortunately, they resurface whenever a stressful situation bordering on immense panic occurs in my life. When I found myself in Athens in 1965 and had to visit the First Aid station, I again felt the same thing. Suddenly, scenes from the anguish I experienced while driving the wounded during the "Dekemvriana" awakened within me and I felt the same trembling immobilization of my body.

Livadia was my first stopover on the way to Florina. Upon arriving at the main square, I was surrounded by ELAS guerrillas who were heartened upon seeing an American flag. In broken English, they began to ask me about the situation in Athens. Only a camera could capture their surprised look when they heard me speak Greek.

"Guys, he's one of us! He's a Greek-American!"

More than ten ELAS guerrillas gathered around my jeep and with inquiring looks they begged for news. I told them the first thing I needed at that very moment was something to eat because I felt drained from hunger.

"Park the jeep on the roadside. We'll take you somewhere to eat."

The man who spoke was about thirty years old and appeared to be the leader of the group of guerrillas. He took me to a tavern, where the food had finished and so the tavern owner prepared a makeshift meal for me. They also offered me a little ouzo. Two or three more guerrillas came into the tavern obviously at the bidding of their commander, who ordered the rest to remain outside.

My arrival quickly became the event of the day and triggered the interest of the British, who sent a major and a captain to meet me and to suggest that I spend the night at their Headquarters.

I declined politely, telling them I had already accepted a proposal of hospitality. Faced with their insistence to not entrust my safety with the ELAS guerrillas, I admit they forced me to abandon my good manners. In the end, they were obliged to leave. Oddly, no one was happy with that development: when I detailed my conversation with the British, the guerrillas did not believe me.

Unfortunately, Greeks are like that and do not trust easily, but I could not fault them after what they had gone through. These guys suffered some losses a few days ago when, feeling dismayed at how things in Athens and Piraeus had evolved, a dozen of them set out to meet their comrades outside the city. On their way, they were attacked by a British bomber that strafed them with sustained fire that dug trenches on the road in order to block their path. Scobie's orders, they were told, prohibited any movements of rebel forces in any direction.

Early next morning, I continued my trip toward Thessaloniki with a stopover at Larissa. There, I met a Greek-American officer of the OSS naval forces whose name I cannot recall and an American officer, Tom Stix, who earlier had been based at Euboea. Both were quite concerned by the filthy game the British were playing. Stix had even cursed them to their faces. They both informed me that a leading communist member, Karageorgis, who was in Volos, had publicly voiced disagreement with the decisions EAM-ELAS took in Athens, which indicated that more alarming developments were in store. So, I decided I should change my itinerary and pass by Volos in order to meet him and learn more. During our discussion, it became obvious that he was quite genuinely upset and was determined to react at the first opportunity.

I left for Thessaloniki the following day. I found the same situation there. Marcos, Bakirtzis and all those who I met and spoke with seemed equally concerned and unable to understand how matters had taken such a turn, for which none of them could offer a reasonable explanation.

General Bakirtzis and his Chief of Staff.

They told me that they looked forward to Macedonia-Thessaloniki EAM-ELAS leaders meeting and making their own assessment of the decisions reached at the Athens headquarters.

In essence, they had entered Thessaloniki against orders from the Athens Headquarters to remain where they were. During the general meeting two days later, however, there was no consensus. Thus, the prevailing view was that they would not attack the British forces camped on the outskirts of Thessaloniki and hesitant to enter the city.

While I was in Macedonia, during the second phase of my mission, I had the opportunity of holding several talks with Bakirtzis, an honorable military officer and a true patriot. I trusted him because he was an intelligent, literate man with sound political judgment and no ulterior motives and personal ambitions. He weighed his words cautiously. Even though he knew with whom he was conversing, he neither avoided me nor tried to provide me with fake and misleading news regarding the current situation. In his view, the Lebanon and Caserta meetings gave rise to grave mistakes and those mistakes were being repeated today, tipping the scales in favor of the reactionary forces.

"What do you think? Did we not make mistakes?"

We were seated on the rocks of the beach at Aretsou, a beautiful fishing village in the suburbs of Thessaloniki. He had invited me to lunch at the home of one his friends and after lunch the two of us stepped outside to take a stroll and chat. I realized he liked talking with me and asking for my opinion. He wanted to find out what people overseas thought about them and whether and how much Greeks throughout the country trusted them.

"General, I'll be frank with you, whether you like it or not. Roughly 70-80 percent of the Greek people living in cities and villages are on the side of EAM. Even so, they are frightfully anxious because those in command are communists. This frightens them. Perhaps without the discipline and organizational capabilities of the communist elements in EAM, the resistance movement might not have managed to attain its objectives until now. All the same, as things have developed through blunders, retaliation and exploitation of events by the reactionaries, it is only natural that people would be skeptical."

He listened carefully without interrupting. Only when I asked him why he had not followed Karageorgis' paradigm in Volos who attacked the British forcing them to abandon the city and to go by ship to Athens, did he turn to me and ask me to get up. We walked along the beach for some time before returning to his friend's house. Now it was his turn to start talking and explaining to me.

"Matters are not nearly as unproblematic as you might see them, Alekos — and I'm not criticizing you for that. In any case, I'm greatly interested in your opinion, which is why I seek to talk with you.

"Anyone who has studied Greek history recognizes how difficult this country is to govern without foreign involvement. This is how it has been governed since the era of the Greek Revolution. But one should not fault only the foreigners for that. Blame should also fall on our shoulders because, whenever divisions arose among us or whenever we encountered difficulties, we rushed to them for assistance. We are doing the same thing today. Mistakes and successive blunders on our part have paved the way for Churchill and the King to call the shots to our detriment.

"You have asked why I did not follow Karageorgis' example in Volos. Have you really considered what might have happened if I had marched into Thessaloniki? I didn't only think of the lives of those who would perish — and certainly those killed wouldn't be only British; Greek blood would have been spilled too. The most dramatic consequence would be, in my own estimation, EAM's own division. Believe me, had that happened, it would have been the worst catastrophe and a terrible failure for our resistance movement."

I marveled at his equanimity with regard to the way he saw things because I knew that, if he so desired, he could enter Thessaloniki in no time and chop off British heads — and yet, he would not do so.

On the following day, however, I asked Vafiadis to tell me his own opinion. I wanted to see whether his opinion coincided with the general's views. Marcos did not mince his words. Since he did not like talking, his answers were, at best, of a few words. He was a very strong and disciplined character, reared by suffering that only Asia Minor refugees had experienced. A man who clearly saw that much darker days lay ahead. He was extremely worried by the ELAS groups which seceded and joined the ranks of SNOF and their leader, Gotchev.

In the meantime, the Varkiza Agreement was signed, forcing ELAS to lay down its arms, but those up in the mountains refused to do so. I distrusted the briefing Daniels gave me as well as that of a British Intelligence Service colonel by the name of Evans, who I met at the home of the former where he remained due to infirmity. When I was told of the particulars, I left for Veroia, where I found out Marcos was pursuing Gotchev and a force of Slavomacedonians who were fighting in order to create an independent Macedonian state.

I remained there for two days trying to hear about the outcome of the operation. I found out that Marcos, in charge of the ELAS force, managed to push back the infamous Gotchev to the area of Lake Prespes from where he was able to re-enter Yugoslav territory. Marcos also told me that the Americans pursued by ELAS, with EDES remnants after the battle against them in Epirus, were taken to safety in Corfu. That was great news which I immediately wired to Athens Headquarters because they worried about the fate of those Americans and had instructed me to investigate the issue. In two days' time, they were back in Athens, without losses.

I met Bakirtzis in a Thessaloniki hospital where two of the seven ELAS guerrillas who had been injured while pursuing Gotchev were being treated. The general spoke to literally nobody. He had been obliged to oversee the disarmament of forces that he had until recently commanded and to bid each of his men farewell, sending them off to their homes, though he knew what was in store. He worked with a leader from the Political Committee of National Liberation (PEEA), named Kikitsis. None of them, not even Markos, had any doubts how they would be treated by Churchill, the British and Papandreou — the latter, in particular, due to his unsubtle personal ambitions.

Like a lightning bolt, a thought crossed my mind: Without the death of Roosevelt, whom the British despised because he stood as an obstacle to their efforts to reinstate the King and also because of his scathing criticism of them, things would have turned out very differently for Greece. Not that he would have permitted the communists to prevail, naturally, but he would have doubtless helped find a solution without bloodshed, recognizing a proper and honorable place for the Resistance and, finally, helping the Greek people elect the government they desired.

During that period, I received instructions from Athens to meet Captain Edson, code named "Bald Eagle," who was in Thessaloniki, and arrange a meeting with Bakirtzis. Before the war, Edson was a historian at the University of Wisconsin. During the war, he was one of the most accomplished assets of the Research and Analysis Division of the OSS in Washington. After the war, despite the fact that the OSS abolished its overseas offices, Edson was dispatched to be at Donovan's order the chief of the Greek Office, in order to file reports to Washington on the conflict between the British and ELAS during the Civil War. Daniels was also at the meeting held at his house at Aretsou. He and Sperling, now chief of intelligence for the Greek Desk, monitored the irredentist movements of SNOF in Macedonia. The Bulgarians declared a bounty on Daniels, with whom, as he wrote in a report, he played "a game of life or death."

Sperling and his radioman visiting Thrace after the liberation.

With my superior, deputy chief of the OSS Mission in Istanbul, Jerome Sperling.
Sperling was an archaeologist who before the war took part in excavations in
Turkey as a member of the American archaeological mission to Troy.

I never learned what they discussed because the next day I received a new order to return to Athens and from there my destination would be Cairo. The order did not state the reasons, but I was certain that my mission was finally drawing to a close and I would return home to America. On these grounds, I requested leave to visit my mother, at Karpathos, whom I had not seen for 28 whole years.

The answer reached me fairly soon, eliciting mixed feelings of joy and anguish, for an adventure that would evidently continue. The opportunity to visit Karpathos would be granted, but not at that specific moment: only after my return to Athens. The reason I was asked to go to Cairo was different from what I had initially supposed. It pertained to an internal financial audit and a citation for my action with the Legion of Merit.

Cairo:
Through Different Eyes

The first thing I felt upon arrival in that mythic city was that the mystique I had known the first time was gone. Heavily-populated military missions had been withdrawn, for the most part. Foreigners were far sparser and their haunts that lent a tone of European glamour were now desolate. The city, with its dusty roads, appeared to have returned to its routine pre-war rhythms. There is no question I viewed matters differently at that time, in part because of my disposition and all I had lived through sequestered for so many months in the most far-flung regions Greece.

I went to our offices to submit my report to Colonel Harry Aldridge, the successor to Captain John Toulmin, the chief of the Cairo OSS office. I did not leave the city immediately afterwards, however. Due to my decoration, I remained there for about three weeks, during which time I met old friends and acquaintances who sought firsthand information regarding the situation in Greece. In the wake of developments in Greece, the British were disgruntled and lots of worthy officers were incarcerated in Middle East concentration camps.

Alexander Georgiades while receiving the Bronze Star Award by the
Chief Mission of OSS Harry Aldridge in Cairo.

Copy

Receipt No. ______________________   Date *July 18, 1944*

This acknowledges receipt of *Two Mixed Gold Pieces*

MGP (No. 2) from *A.M. Georgiades*

this represents unexpended funds returned to OSS; said funds having been

advanced to *him* in accordance with Vo.No. *611*

Accounting, CREDIT: Signed *H. George*
Special Funds Officer, Istanbul

00 Advance	
01 Pers Serv	BRANCH *North Base*
02 Travel	
03	MISSION
04 Communications	
05 Rents, Util, etc	
06 Other Contr	VALUE L.T. *23.60*
08 Sup, Mat, etc	
09 Equipment	
10 Accts Adv	*23.60* *$ 13.07*

Mine French.   *$ 6.5335*

Receipt for the return of unspent golden sovereigns from Georgiades to the OSS Office in Cairo after the completion of the first phase of his mission to Evros. His reputation as an incorruptible man was noted by the US military authorities and was seriously taken into account for his distinctions when he returned to America, July 8, 1944.

I literally shuddered… It was inconceivable for me that the British had neutralized competent and valiant officers with whom they had fought alongside during the battle against the Axis. In the final analysis, these officers were not their own but officers from foreign forces. How had Papandreou accepted this? How had he acquiesced to such great dishonor?

Even worse, all democratically-minded officers were jailed and promotions were granted only to pro-royalist and to pro-Metaxas officers who had been appointed to pivotal leadership posts in the Armed Forces. While in Cairo, I managed to confirm information I had learned but until then found difficult to believe: namely, that the same thing had occurred in Athens, where some officers who sympathized with ELAS were imprisoned, while others were confined in various military camps.

Relieved of the stresses of Greece and my mission, I was able to find my own pace in Cairo's different rhythms and combine many of the puzzle pieces that had engaged my mind in the past, but which, due to inadequate time and information, I had never sorted out.

In Cairo.

Returning to Athens, I received a much-desired furlough to visit my mother in Karpathos. I flew to Iraklion, Crete, and from there via Siteia boarded the caique of a relative, who sailed regularly to Kassos, to my birthplace, my beloved Karpathos.

Return to Karpathos

Like a modern day Ulysses, I arrived one twilight at my island on a wind-battered caique of a Cretan relative. Twenty-eight years and some months had passed since I left. While firmly gripping the mast, and with Karpathos now in view in the distance, I felt as if I were dreaming and that none of this was truly happening.

The wind whistled maniacally around me, the waves grew ever deeper and darker as sunlight slipped away and yet, despite the cold, I refused to descend to the hold for protection. I wished to embrace the magic of my return. My emotion-laden heart felt as if it might burst.

I remembered the freezing cold of New York when I first set foot there in February 1916. Bitter winds had blown there also, but here the winds seemed to speak to me in words of both pity and joy: as if to seek reasons why my return took so long and yet simultaneously to welcome me back — me, Alekos, son of Varvaroula, the only one who remained alive to keep our home.

We reached the shoreline with great difficulty. I saw two men there pulling up some improvised nets, apparently preparing to cast their next one. I could not recognize them, nor could they recognize me.

"So much the better," I thought to myself, for it was not the right time for greetings. Emotion and fatigue had triumphed, leaving me looking frail compared to them.

I straightened my back, took a deep breath and asked the two men where they were from and whether they could conduct me to my village.

"And you?" one of the men asked. "Who are you and whom do you seek?" Though only one of them asked me, it was as if he snatched the questions directly from the mouth of the other.

I hesitated.

"The grandson of Sakellis, the priest," I answered. I still wonder why I did not state the names of my parents instead. It was not because my father had died, since I already knew that. Nor did I avoid doing so from dread they might utter something distressing about my mother. But in citing my grandfather the priest, deceased for so many years, it almost felt like warding off evil.

"Ah," they said together, "So you're the son of Varvaroula, eh? The American? Alexandros?"

Three questions, each with an identical answer.

"Yes, it is I!" Despite not knowing who they were, I hugged them. For me, they were Karpathians and that in itself was enough.

Fortunately, they were not overly inquisitive. They did not ask for the reasons behind my visit nor why I had chosen this time of year.

"Well, imagine that… Only yesterday I saw your mother in her vegetable garden. And today I see you! Does she know you're here?" "Certainly not," I said in a somewhat austere tone of voice. "How could she have learned it?" Relieved by the news that my mother was alive, my spirits were elevated. I felt at least like a king.

The route to the village in a dilapidated Chevrolet seemed to take an eternity as it creaked and groaned at every curve as if each turn would be its last. Nonetheless, it succeeded in ascending the mountain.

"My village! I finally see it!"

Though night was falling, I could still easily make out the surrounding houses. Nothing had changed. At least, so it seemed.

From within our house, there was a flickering light. The silence was unbelievable. When the noise from the jalopy's engine subsided — perhaps the island's sole means of transportation —, I could hear a night bird somewhere nearby.

With my heart throbbing in my chest and ready to break, I knocked softly on the wooden door.

I heard footsteps. Then, with a distinctive rattle, the iron latch was lifted and the door opened. Standing before me was my mother.

"Mother! It's me, Alexandros!"

I all but fell on her, hugging tightly her thin body with both arms.

Upon loosening my embrace, I saw her looking me over, wordlessly, with tear-filled eyes. A deep sigh came from within her and, with words that pricked my heart, she said:

"Alekos, my child. You have grown so much, my boy, and it passed me by. Life can be so cruel."

She grabbed me from the hand as if I were still a little child and led me inside. She sat me down on a stone bench, covered in decorative Karpathian bedclothes. It was exactly opposite her bed, which had been prepared for her night's rest.

She averted her gaze and then glanced about.

"Do you remember our home, Alekos?"

"How could I forget, mother? Our home and our island are virtually etched within me."

I stretched out my arms to take her hands in mine. As if embarrassed, she had crossed her arms in front of her, between her chest and abdomen, holding back her woven Karpathian nightgown.

I gently caressed her hands, knotted with calluses from endless hours of manual work. I kissed her hands as if kissing an icon and then stood for a few minutes studying her wrinkled face. Indeed, one might imagine I was reading there the history of my birthplace.

"Mother," I said. "Oh, my mother."

Words failed me. I could find neither the words to say first nor those to say afterwards. Time seemed to have stood as still as the stone walls of the house.

"Will you eat something, son? We were all alone in this house. Everyone has gone. Let me get up and prepare something for you. I had boiled potatoes for myself, but I ate them."

Her last words caused her some muffled and barely-contained nervous laughter.

I left her alone in the small kitchen, at the other end of the main room, to prepare my food and went outside into the small courtyard of the house. I looked above me into the boundless star-filled sky. It was the same sky I gazed upon as a child. Memories from when I left my island had been carried away in my mind much like a thief with his loot.

My venerable mother tapped lightly two or three times on the window and I understood that I should go inside. That night, I ate the tastiest tomatoes of my life and the sweetest bread, lightly smeared with a splash of oil and a pinch of oregano.

After sitting across from me and watching me while I ate, she rose to prepare me a place to sleep in the adjacent room.

When I finished my evening meal, I bade her good night with the promise that early in the morning we would wake up and I would tell her everything.

I left my door ajar to watch over her. I was fearful of her unrest, aware of her frailty.

She slept immediately. I understood it from the rhythm of her breathing. I remained awake for hours, immersed in my thoughts.

In total, I stayed with my mother for thirty-two days. For as long as I live, I shall never forget that first morning. It was as though I awoke in an enchanted place. The light of day had a radiance I had forgotten in my years living abroad. When I opened the window, the scents of nature flooded the room and, despite the previous day's six hour journey from Siteia to there, I felt an unexpected sense of well-being.

Mother had risen much earlier and already was outside in her vegetable garden. I saw her bent over something, but could not make out what it was.

I went through the rest of the house. I wanted solitude to look it over in peace. In every corner, there were cherished and beloved faces, as if time itself was undisturbed and our souls alone were filled with wrinkles. Even the old clock that my father once brought from Athens had stopped. It showed lost hours, I thought.

I was again observing my mother from the little window of the kitchen. She had raised her body now and made an effort to hold herself upright. From where I was standing, she could not see me and I could watch her undisturbed. I realized she was mumbling to herself. I thought that undeterred as she was by apprehensions of misfortune, this elderly lady had raised children and grandchildren and now remained alone in life without expecting anything, except to see me again.

During my stay, we did nothing else but talk and visit relatives in my village. We went to the graves of my father and my grandfathers. From there, I had a better view directly below to the sea which was full of waves. When I was small, I called them "little lambs," since they were white and breaking on the shoreline one after another. Here, on my island, I learned to count. It was mathematics of the sea.

Apart from her persistent questions about why I was there and why I had not brought luggage with me, it was impossible to tell her the truth. I told her only that I was asked to help as a translator in Cairo for the Americans who were following the war in Greece. She did not seem to understand, but it was probably better for me that way.

The days passed swiftly. When the final one arrived and I had to depart, my soul was so burdened that I made a great effort not to show it.

We sat for a while next to the fireplace, which burned day and night, waiting for the car to ascend to collect us. She insisted on accompanying me down to the port. I did not want this, since it would make the separation more difficult, but faced with her persistence I could not do otherwise.

We looked at each other in silence for a few minutes. Our mouths were filled with silence and our eyes were full of promises we knew we could not keep.

Startled, we jumped at the sound of the jalopy. I grabbed my military bag with one hand and held it by the other. I asked the driver if he could take both of us.

"Just as we agreed yesterday," he said.

I was unaware of this. I turned to look toward my mother and the driver cast me a sly glance with a wink. She had arranged this on her own.

During the descent, I was trying to collect mental images at every twist and turn. I wanted to take them all with me. It was so uncertain if or when I might return here.

The procedure was quick. We would follow the same route to Siteia, with a stopover at Kassos.

The time for farewells had arrived. I embraced my venerable mother and kissed her face and hands as if she were a holy icon. Then, in one stride, I boarded the caique. As the boat pulled away from the shore, I noticed her waving her scarf. A bracing splash of seawater hit me and it felt as though the history of my birthplace itself washed over me.

In the background, as her form began to slip away, I swear God seemed so alone. And so did she. She was already eighty-two years old. I was sure we would never see one another again.

My whole life was like a musical chord. This encounter with my mother interposed a third tone.

My Third Return to Macedonia

After returning from Karpathos, I remained in Athens for a few days. The situation was in steady decline. People were famished and fears of retaliation after the end of the first round of the Civil War were rampant. Everyone I met in Athens and Piraeus, whether friends or foes, were equally desperate. They had lost all hope for a return to a normal life after the war because matters had been driven toward an onerous impasse.

My heart ached when I thought that ultimately Greeks had to set out on their own Odyssey at different times and eras. And now they had to do it again.

As for me, I had only to wait for my transfer order to return to America. Instead, however, I was ordered to travel again to Macedonia. I was based in Thessaloniki and stayed at the same house where I used to live at Panorama. My job was to cover the entire region up to the Evros. After the Varkiza Agreement, the situation was turbulent and matters were getting out of hand.

I was told I would be working together with John Koukos, another Greek-American from a small town near Pittsburgh. He was an affable and joyful kid, who proved to be quite good company. He worried about his pregnant wife who was about to deliver. Sometimes, when our lives were at risk, I took better care of him than I did myself, since I did not want him to be harmed and his child to be without a father.

Wherever John and I went, we heard and saw the same things. Terrified people whose faces mirrored their fears. In villages, assaults and murders were a daily routine. Somewhere on the outskirts of Serres, a villager spoke to us about his personal experience that must not have been much different from that of others. He told us that one day as he was heading home from his farm, armed men stopped him in the middle of the street and asked him what his political convictions were. The unfortunate man realized that, if he told them what they wanted to hear, they would go away without harming him. He stood still and sized things up.

He was unfeigned and for a moment the notion to tell them the truth crossed his mind. To tell them, in other words, that all he cared for was to live in peace with his family and be able to protect them. However, he knew that even this would earn him a bashing. The only thing they wanted to hear was that he was with them. And that is what he did, guessing that this would please them.

One should understand that, in the circumstances, the fear Greek people experienced was greater than their fear of the German and Bulgarian occupations, both notorious for their cruelty. It was also completely outrageous that the police George Papandreou organized — prompted, of course, by the British as soon as he returned to Greece — remained indifferent to these unfortunate crimes. Even worse, when they intervened, they supported the pro-Right Wing paramilitary organizations. The OPLA members, a national militia and EAM's armed branch tasked with protecting citizens' security founded during the German Occupation, were ruthlessly and relentlessly persecuted by the police. As a result, they struck back and, thereby, bloodshed was perpetuated.

Terror reigned everywhere and no one knew if they would return home after work. Only in Evros had the situation become substantially calmer. Following the Varkiza accord, there were outbreaks there too, though few of them were truly fierce. For the most part, the rhythms of normal life had returned.

The climate of merciless and abiding persecution made escaping to the mountains appear as the sole solution for most of the followers of EAM and its armed branch ELAS. It was exactly then that the second round of the Civil War began: a period marked by the withdrawal of British forces from the country as the economy of the erstwhile empire foundered, to the point it could not continue its guardianship of tiny Greece. And so we took over, announced the Truman Doctrine and launched the program of economic relief of Europe through the Marshall Plan, which, of course, included Greece.

John and I stayed in Greece for another six months in all. During that period, we roamed the countryside from Thrace to Epirus and from Epirus to the Peloponnese. We were often touched by countless emotions, while we observed the strength, the magnificence and above all the decency with which the Greek people tried to survive through scarcity and with almost incxistent public utility infrastructure, a total absence of running water and supply of electrical power. Still, famine was the most painful and harrowing of all other hardships as it affected infants and young children in particular.

Out of the several incidents I witnessed, one in particular I recall with clarity and it remains permanently etched in my memory: a young girl who died in front of my eyes, whose expression, until the last instant, was a refusal to accept the fact of death, despite knowing death itself was upon her. This happened in Thessaloniki, in the square outside the Hotel Mediterranean. John and I found ourselves there as people began to gather.

We supposed a protest rally was about to take place. Later, we learned the rally was held to celebrate the anniversary of the Liberation. Before long, thousands of people from all over the city filled the entire square. It was not difficult to see numerous policemen in the crowd, many of whom were in civilian clothes. At some point, a girl, about seventeen years old, clashed with the head of the police force when he asked her not to sing Resistance songs and called her a "damn Slavo-communist." She answered that she was proud to be a communist and called him a "dirty fascist." For him, that was too much. He drew his knife and slaughtered her in front of our eyes. I heard him say: "We knew who you were. One of these days, we were going to catch you."

"Fascist!" was the girl's last word. In mere moments, a huge crowd attacked him and tried to lynch the cowardly killer. Suddenly, as if out of nowhere, soldiers, policemen and armed security men in civilian clothes appeared and encircled the offender and, with their guns protruding at the ready, were clearly prepared to shoot to kill.

Above the fracas, I clearly heard the voice of an officer order his men to open fire. John and I rushed to bring the jeep closer for any eventuality. I parked in a side street and walked to the main street to see what was happening, telling John to remain inside the jeep to protect himself. Only two days before, we had learned that his wife had given birth to a boy.

At the first corner, I heard shots being fired and saw the crowd running away in all directions, trying to save themselves. Beside me, on the stoop of a doorway, two soldiers were kneeling and shooting at the people.

"Halt your fire!" I said. "Can't you see that you are firing against unarmed people?"

Although baffled, they both did as I said. They saw an American officer in his military uniform speaking to them in Greek and, as if by some miracle, they stopped shooting.

In front of us, on the pavement, two men and a woman were wounded and yelling for help. Along with two British soldiers — who appeared at that moment from who knows where —, I ran in their direction. I shouted to John, who had gotten out of the jeep, alarmed by the sound of gunfire to bring the jeep closer, and asked one of the demonstrators to tell me how to get to the hospital. It was not difficult to find the hospital. What was difficult was to enter it.

Upon arriving at the gate, the security guard told me he had orders to forbid entrance to everyone. I asked him to call the hospital director and, when he refused to do so, I started shouting so loudly that a middle-aged nurse came out to see what was happening. She repeated the same line, despite the fact she could see the two wounded men and the woman who was bleeding heavily. I felt so tense and my blood pressure soaring, I thought I would die on the spot.

"Lady, I couldn't care less about the orders you have," I yelled, asking her to call a doctor, while we moved forward with me carrying the woman in my arms, as John along with the security guard carried the other two men, who were so pale as if half dead.

Within a few minutes, and after all within earshot had heard me curse them in both Greek and English, a doctor finally appeared and hastened to make excuses, saying he was delayed, but that he was the only doctor on call and could not attend to all of them. But when he saw my American military uniform, his became wing-footed and before we knew it all three wounded were on surgical beds and receiving first aid. After John and I saw they were being carefully treated and we were no longer needed, we left the hospital and headed back to the square.

The crowd had dispersed. Only the dead and wounded were lying on the ground. Soldiers and policemen were walking among and over them, nudging them with their feet to see whether they were alive or dead. Next to the slain girl, there were six dead people and many more wounded around them. When the officer in charge saw us, he gave us a sermon saying the communists were to be blamed for the massacre. He concluded his short speech saying, "We'll devour them all!"

A wave of profound disappointment and despair instantly engulfed me. Seeing the hatred of those people, I was convinced this country could not stand again on its feet free unless it managed to conquer its internal adversary. Reconciliation seemed entirely unimaginable under such circumstances. I strongly doubted whether there would be a politician from the younger generation to make the Greek people believe in reconciliation and then implement it.

Following the fall of the colonels' dictatorship and the emergence of the student movement that was the vanguard of the anti-dictatorial struggle, there may be hope that new leaders will rise who will be vastly different from their corrupt pre-war peers who are responsible for the catastrophic course things have taken. The only good thing the junta did was to abolish the monarchy, which caused only tribulations for Greece.

I remember that, whenever as a child I was in distress, a poem came to mind that I learned in elementary school in Karpathos. It is called "The Rock and the Wave." It tells of the way anger empowers the wave battering the rock which remains serene and in fact jeers at the wave because it believes it cannot possibly harm it. But gradually the wave manages to eat away at the rock until one day the rock is shattered into a thousand pieces. Whenever I feel hopeless at the faint steps of progress people take, in their effort to achieve their humanistic ideals, I bring to mind that poem and hope is reborn within me.

I have to acknowledge that, while I was in Macedonia for a third time, I got the chance to meet Evripidis Bakirtzis several times. Sometimes, he would come to our offices and sometimes we met either at Aretsou, in Thessaloniki, or at the house of his sister, a polite lady whose married name was Dimitriadis. Her husband, then deceased, was a renowned doctor in Thessaloniki. Her daughter Lilika was the General's niece and the most beloved one. During one of my visits, I was acquainted with two friends of hers, Aliki, who was a teacher, and Eleni, a dynamic young lawyer, who after the war defended in court many of those who the State Security falsely accused of dozens of murders. She did not collect fees for her work — after all the defendants did not have the money to pay her —, but she accepted only travel costs from those who could pay because not all the trials were held in Thessaloniki.

The general was, like Stathatos, the most incorruptible Greek military officer I met during my entire stay in Greece that lasted many months. He was a genuine patriot who commanded everyone's respect, including his enemies. I remember him telling me that, after Varkiza and the arrests of leading ELAS members, he should have been in fact arrested as he disobeyed Scobie's orders and traveled to Thessaloniki with Marcos. But he was not.

"Aleko," I still recall him telling me, "Varkiza was a pure act of treachery by the KKE leaders. It left all of us exposed to the persecuting authorities, who found themselves free to fabricate against us whatever charges suited them. Just look at the dozens of fighters who were jailed and now wait to stand trial. Will they make it? I very much doubt it. Most will not survive and will die in the wretched holding cells where they are detained."

In the end, it did not take them long to arrest him as well and exile him to Ikaria. He remained dignified to the end, preferring death to disgrace. One night, he cooked for a few friends, likewise in exile, and they dined all together. He seemed to be in good spirits, but it was evident he had made up his mind. He committed suicide that same night. The locals spoke of a strange visit by unknown people who sailed near the island on a boat most probably with intent to kill him. He preempted them. I learned all those details in 1965, when I returned to Greece. I tried in vain to communicate with his family when I heard the news of his death while I was in America. They did not respond. I still remember how saddened I was when I learned how this magnificent man died.

But let me now turn again to what I was telling you about my days in Thessaloniki because I want to say a few more things concerning my meeting with Woodhouse. In any event, the impression I had about him before we met was simply reinforced after our meeting.

The reason why we met was John Charakas from Chicago. He was head of the Greek War Relief Association whom I got to know in Cairo and was in Thessaloniki when Spyros Skouras, of the Skouras Brothers family, was also there. Skouras ran the same Office for Greek Aid in America code-named "Vulture."

I had only a casual acquaintance with Spyros because my personal friend was his brother George Skouras, with whom I worked sending poultry and livestock when I returned to America after the war.

Like all important visitors in that period, he stayed at the Hotel Mediterranean. The three of us had a lengthy discussion regarding the situation in Greece and reached the same conclusions. While I was leaving the room, he asked me to come and see him again on the following day for a meeting with influential persons, as he called them, because he believed that it would be useful for them to hear my first-hand account of events.

He told me that bigwig Chris Woodhouse would be there, too. Obviously he had heard rumors about the notorious British man and his character. He turned out to be one of the biggest anti-Hellenes of all times and I am sorry that his role has not been elucidated and adequately explained, even belatedly, because facts speak for themselves regarding the character of this man and his arrogant stance towards Greece and the Greeks.

I will explain below what I mean. But let me begin from the first and only meeting we had.

He came into the room where we, the American delegation, had already taken our seats, escorted by two or three men whose role I could not determine, as they remained silent throughout the meeting. He had the appearance of a typical English aristocrat: blond and tall, pretentious. Probably on purpose, he spoke with a strong Oxford accent and was visibly bored as if he were granting us a favor by even being with us, the provincial Americans.

We were properly introduced. When he heard my name, he could no longer hide his feelings. He was aware that I was gazing at him. I watched him turn around to look at me and at the same time take his eyes off me in a show of contempt.

I was delighted and could not conceal my own feelings. You see, I ridiculed them at Evros. How could they forgive me? They lost more than sixty operatives of their Intelligence Service there, while we, that is I, who had crossed the River fourteen times to lay the groundwork for cooperation with the guerrillas for James Kellis' mission to blow up the bridges of Svilengrad, in Bulgaria, and Alexandroupolis, did not lose a single man. Furthermore, we uncovered their real goal, which was to restore the King in Greece. They were so obsessed with the restoration of the monarchy that, if it served their interests, they would not object to a King governing Greece even if the Germans continued their occupation.

It goes without saying that during our discussion we remained secluded in the same small room for hours without hiding our mutual antipathy. I wonder, for the sake of the argument, if I were indeed a gullible American, why did his British phlegm disappear? I swear by God I would like to read one day the reports he wrote about me in his capacity as chief of the British Intelligence in Greece.

After they had left, Skouras turned to me and asked, "What's going on between the two of you, Alex?"

"What can I tell you?" I replied. "The man is 'one of a kind.' God made him and then broke the mold. At least, that is what I want to believe for the good of this country."

I told him more things. Skouras appeared to be chagrined and laughed only when he heard me mutter to myself: "I wonder how different things would be for this country had the sister of a friend of mine not provided him shelter after he parachuted wounded in 1942, leaving him to the mercy of the Germans."

Woodhouse turned out to be a fateful man for Greece. And this is not, unfortunately, only my opinion. Before me, Captain Winston Ehrgott, in Cairo, had denounced this ambitious Brit of deliberately delaying transmits of his reports and using codes that Cairo could not decipher. This, by the way, was an additional term the British had raised, that is they demanded to have all American cables go through their signals. Roosevelt, from what I was told, complained more than once to Churchill about the hurdles posed by the Intelligence to Americans. But he was unyielding and insisted on the Brits having the main role in the Balkans, which they regarded their own territory. Even when the President made a last-minute appeal to the British prime minister using his trump card called Donovan, Churchill said that, although he admired the general, he nonetheless thought he would not be able to make heads or tails in the Balkans.

It was obvious now that the English-American rivalry, initially evident in June 1942, albeit subtly, when the OSS was established, grew into an open dispute between two main allies one year later. It was not difficult to guess who the winner would be. Initially, Woodhouse managed to get rid of his superior, Brigadier General Meyers, who was accused of being pro-EAM and pro-ELAS because he tried to fly to Cairo heading a group of guerrillas to normalize relations between EAM-ELAS and the King. Then, he eliminated our guy, Ehrgott, aka 'Wink', who was also accused of being a fellow-traveler. Ehrgott was a fine horse trainer and tried to train guerrillas to handle the horses the Italians left behind when they fled Greece with the aim of setting up a cavalry regiment of ELAS for the war.

In one of my meetings with Ehrgott, he told me that in his latest report to Cairo before his discharge he openly expressed his antipathy for and lack of trust in Woodhouse, whom he described as an arrogant person who had not worked once in his lifetime, while he despised the Greek people who, unlike him, fought tooth and nail to survive.

Group Captain Hooling, who participated in Operation Feather 3 in Western Macedonia, suffered the same destiny as British Colonel Nicholas Hammond accused him of spending too long delivering speeches in the towns and cities and taking the side of the guerrillas.

It was crystal clear that the British were interested not in the war but in the restoration of the monarchy in Greece. News from Greece reached the Greek king in Cairo at the speed of light as he protested to Ambassador MacVeagh daily that the Americans in Greece were bent upon undercutting his royal power and dignity and sternly asked that their activities be restricted.

One should add to all these a story among many more others that I recently read and that seems to be true because it was narrated by New Zealand Major General Bernard Freyberg, the overall commander of allied forces in Crete. I am sorry to say that the British policy did not only have to do with people. According to the major and commander of New Zealand's forces in the Battle of Crete, when the German soldiers were being parachuted, he rushed to meet Woodhouse and found him having his English breakfast unperturbed. He pointed to the sky, which had grown dark from the large numbers of the German parachutists, most of whom were landing dead from the guns of Cretans and Allies, but Woodhouse merely told him to sit down and enjoy the morning tea with him. What sangfroid this man displayed. In another book, I read that on the eve of the German attack the British decided to have a third airport built at Maleme, on which the German combat aircraft landed and which served them better than the other two at Iraklion and Rethymnon.

I wonder if historians will research all those events in the future and provide answers or if the Cold War monster will swallow it all up as if it were the Minotaur.

I do not think Woodhouse himself will do it, though he poses as a historian and has built a reputation around himself. Besides, he does nothing to conceal his loathing of the Greeks. I heard that, after being received by Brigadier General Stylianos Pattakos in Athens, he later told, obviously because of his interlocutor's inanity, an audience of students in Oxford that included several Americans, that his impression of the discussion was that there would have made little difference if he had held it with then US Vice President Spiro Agnew instead of the perjurer colonel.

Of course, I am not defending the Republicans, for whom I never voted, and certainly not the dictators in Greece. However, I want to remind my readers of what I said in the beginning and in fact, if I am not mistaken, it was Aeschylus, the classical Greek tragic dramatist, who wrote: "In war, truth is the first casualty." It is true that many things that occurred during the war are today presented in a completely skewed fashion.

Return to America

When travel orders were finally issued for me to return to America, I was greatly relieved. I flew to Cairo and from there to Casablanca where I was literally stuck waiting, with other Americans, to return home.

For an entire month, I was indifferent to all and sundry and played poker night and day. Then, one day I got lucky: one of our military aircraft needed a radio operator and I was able to embark. After stopovers in Brazil and Miami, I finally landed at Andrews Field, in Washington, D.C.

Alex in Washington D.C.

I went to the military Staff Office to submit my report. I doubt whether anyone will ever be permitted to read that report.

Today, I still remember several of the events I described in the report, as I kept my own notes after exiting the Staff Office. Doing so was made easier, of course, by the fact that I was asked to answer specific questions.

ACHIEVEMENTS IN THE FIELD

1. Operated for a period of thirty months, without the loss of a single man, in an area where two Allied missions had previously failed. These Allied missions had lost more than 60 men in the attempt.

2. Crossed the Turkish-German border 14 times, and had two encounters with the Germans, with no casualties.

3. Crossed the Bulgarian-German border twice, was on one occasion surrounded by the Bulgarians and escaped only under cover of darkness and because of the Bulgarians' ignorance of our strength.

4. Uncovered a Bulgarian spy ring operating over the Turkish border from Evros as far as Istanbul and Ankara. Twenty-two of this ring were arrested by the Turks at Edirne and Istanbul.

5. Discovered that three Turkish officers from the UZUNCOPRU garrison were betraying our movements to the Germans. All three were arrested by Turkish security.

6. Gained the wholehearted cooperation of the Turkish General Safceok, commander of the Turkish army in Thrace, making it possible for me to operate and move freely in a closely guarded Turkish military region and to operate along the border in Turkish uniform.

7. Was instrumental in preventing much bloodshed in the Evros region by prevailing upon both political factions to refrain from fighting each other and to direct their energies against the enemy.

8. Exposed and helped to bring about the downfall of Odysseas, hostile guerrilla leader who had carried on a campaign of violence and terrorism.

9. Transported over the border from Istanbul tons of medical supplies for the guerrillas and for the civilian population.

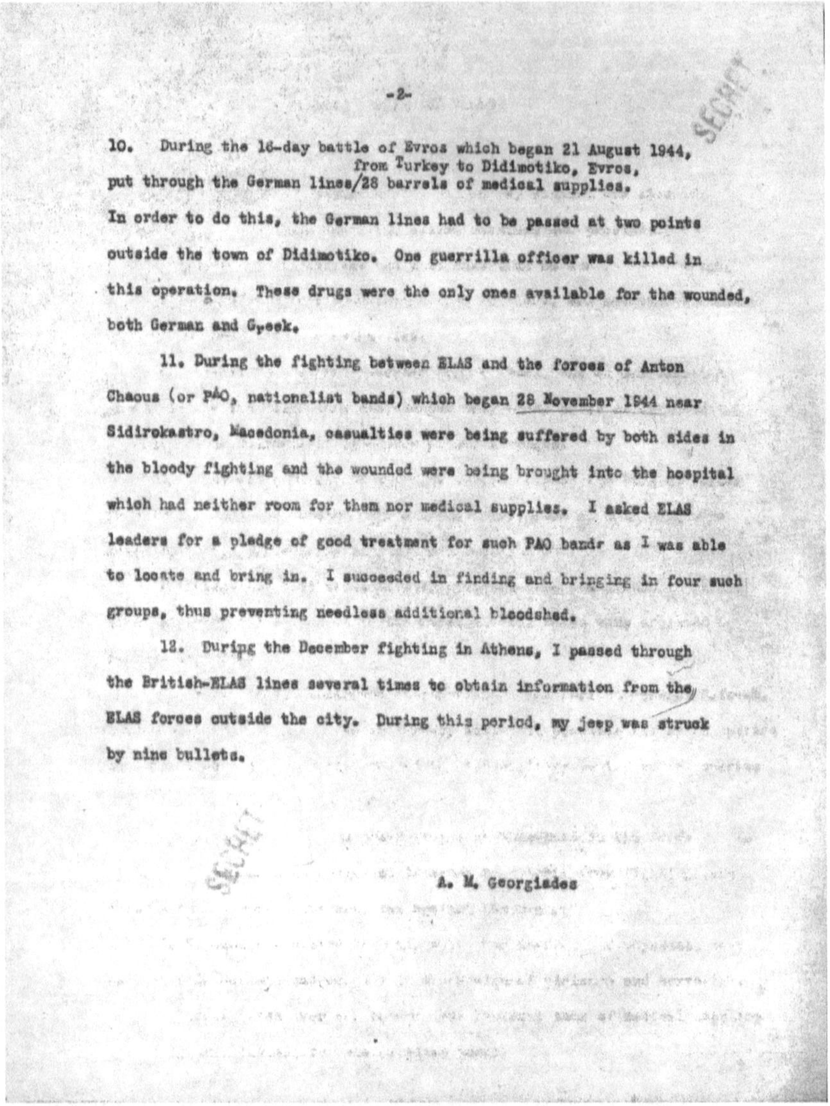

-2-

10.   During the 16-day battle of Evros which began 21 August 1944,
from Turkey to Didimotiko, Evros,
put through the German lines/28 barrels of medical supplies.
In order to do this, the German lines had to be passed at two points
outside the town of Didimotiko. One guerrilla officer was killed in
this operation. These drugs were the only ones available for the wounded,
both German and Greek.

11. During the fighting between ELAS and the forces of Anton
Chaous (or PAO, nationalist bands) which began 28 November 1944 near
Sidirokastro, Macedonia, casualties were being suffered by both sides in
the bloody fighting and the wounded were being brought into the hospital
which had neither room for them nor medical supplies. I asked ELAS
leaders for a pledge of good treatment for such PAO bands as I was able
to locate and bring in. I succeeded in finding and bringing in four such
groups, thus preventing needless additional bloodshed.

12. During the December fighting in Athens, I passed through
the British-ELAS lines several times to obtain information from the
ELAS forces outside the city. During this period, my jeep was struck
by nine bullets.

A. M. Georgiades

A secret document that Georgiades filed upon his return to Washington D.C. informing his superiors about his achievements. It consists of thirteen points. He starts like "within a period of thirty months I operated without the loss of a single man, in an area where the Allied missions (he insinuates the British Intelligence) had lost more than 60 men in the attempt".

When those matters that are secret today become available for everyone to read and for historians to write a true account of events in Greece, I will, no doubt, be long departed.

My mission lasted 30 months, which was quite exceptional because the maximum for serving in the same post was six months. The chief impediments to a lengthy stay were not only fatigue and local conditions, but also psychological factors, owing to our origins, which was the main criterion for our recruitment. My case was an obvious exception.

Even today, I remember how Spyridon Kaponis, code-named "Chicago," who served under Kellis, told me, years after the war, that, after working with ELAS in Northern Greece for a period of two months, he cracked up. During one of our meetings, he recollected what he thought was his worst day during that period:

"One day, the Germans were after us for hours. With my patience running out, I grabbed the machine gun from the hands of the loyal ELAS escort assigned for my protection, asked him to hold the ammunition belt for me and stared shooting in the air frantically.

"I swear to God I was prepared to shoot at anything that moved around me. Fortunately, Athens stopped me, grabbing my arm and telling me, 'Calm down, Gus. We will be out of here soon.'

"I yelled at him: 'I can't stand this shitty war any longer! I'll blow all those bastards sky-high! Please, let's get out of here now!'

"Realizing I was overwrought and beside myself, Athens held me by the neck to immobilize me, but so forcefully that the pain helped me get over the shock.

"What can I tell you, Alekos," he remarked. "We had rough times up there. You can understand what I mean because you lived through it, too."

"But what about others?" he wondered with heartache. "What about our children? Will they ever learn the truth?"

Today, I feel like him as I write this book. I want my children and the whole world to learn the truth, to stop lending credence to a version of that war written by those who tailor events to fit their purposes.

One fact that has been objectively recorded, for instance, is the failure of the British and the Intelligence Service at Evros, where they lost about 60 of their fighters to German gunfire. In contrast, we Americans, and I personally, managed to cross over the river 14 times and operate within the Greek territory without any losses whatsoever — not even when the Germans got wind of me and I had to engage in combat with them twice. Moreover, I also managed to enter Bulgarian territory twice and made a narrow escape thanks to the darkness and the Bulgarians' inability to deal with our military superiority.

Some incidents I did not include in my original story at Edirne.

Just before I was to pick up James Kellis and his radio operators to escort them to the mountains and the ELAS in Evros I took Kellis to the Greek consulate to meet Kambalouris the Edirne consul who was staying now at the Constantinople Greek consulate. While there Kambalouris who by now was very much put out about developments at Edirne and made the statement that my love for Greece was questionable or some remarks to that effect. So I told him about his own interest for Greece pointing out that all the while I was there he or his assistants never once cared to send something even to their friends in Evros since he knew I had the consulate of Constantinople by a lady secretary there filling numerous prescriptions from Evros people given to me by the doctors there which I paid for. He got angry and passed some remarks that also got me up and we created quite a scene that caused people in the consulate to gather to see what was going on. In my anger I made the statement that I would slap him in the face but I couldn't do it since he was feminine enough to paint his face like a harlot. It was known by everyone that he actually paint his face & lip stick.

The first page of Georgiades' personally drafted notes referring to the behavior of N. Kampalouris, Greek Consul General in Adrianople, during their meeting with the Kellis team in the Greek Consulate in Istanbul. The ensuing squabble was so fierce that the consulate secretary took the initiative to close the doors of all adjacent offices and remove the staff. The chasm between the two men was profound. Georgiades found obstacles constantly in his effort to accomplish his mission, while Kampalouris, in cooperation with Raphael in Ankara, worked for the Intelligence Service, collecting, as Georgiades claimed, fees for their services.

Furthermore, I managed to uncover a network of dangerous Bulgarian spies who operated along Evros, Istanbul and Ankara. Twenty-two of them were arrested by the Turks in Adrianople and Istanbul, literally dismantling that ring.

Another major success was when we disclosed that three Turkish military officers belonging to the unit guarding *Uzun Köprü*, the "Long Bridge" at the Greek-Turkish borders, had informed the Germans of our location. Of course, all three were arrested straightaway. The most important development for me was when I was able to gain the confidence of General Seftcheck, Commander of the Turkish Force in Thrace. Thanks to him, I was able to roam freely across an area controlled strictly by the Turkish armed forces attired in Turkish military uniform.

Something no one can dispute is that I was able to stop the civil bloodshed at Evros, reconcile the warring factions and have them join forces against the common enemy, that is, the Germans and their Bulgarian collaborators. Odysseus' removal as a leader of EAM of Thrace and his eventual execution by his comrades helped enormously because he spread terror and violence in the Evros region, making people walk away from the Resistance Front in doubt about its true aims. That is why he was executed by his own comrades.

It is no secret that I risked my life many more times than did the guerrillas themselves. During various phases of our cooperation, I was at risk because they expressed deep suspicion and even questioned the genuine reasons I was there. Whether one believes it or not, I transported dozens of tons of pharmaceutical materials to them and to non-combatants, saving the lives of many people and young children — many of whom suffered from malaria. Twenty-eight shipments of medical and pharmaceutical materials were transported from Turkey to Didymoteichon throughout the battle that started in August 1944 and lasted for 16 days before the Germans abandoned the area in defeat. It was then that we lost, outside Didymoteichon, one of the guerrillas who helped us go through German blockades.

Suffice to say that the aforesaid material was not used only for those wounded on our side, but also for the Germans. Following my appeal to the ELAS leaders, we provided the same humanitarian aid to Tsaus Anton fighters who were injured during the mopping up operations attempted against the guerrillas in November-December 1944. Guerrillas and traitors were given medical aid lying side by side, which was a superb opportunity to remedy the hatred so successfully cultivated by the British and their Intelligence Service, as a result of which they managed to divide the Greek people and lead them to bloodshed.

I lived through the results of the British policy overwhelmingly in Athens, when the "Dekemvriana" events broke out and the civil war started. I risked my life again on two occasions. Luckily, the nine bullets shot in my direction only pierced though my jeep. I had just returned from Thessaloniki, during the last days of November, waiting for new travel orders, most likely to return to Cairo and from there to America. One morning, while driving along Panepistimiou Street, wearing the American military uniform, with the American flag waving in the front of the car, I saw a bunch of elementary school children crossing the street and singing resistance songs, while just on the opposite side British snipers were taking aim at them and preparing to fire. I stopped the car immediately and went out screaming at the soldiers to halt their fire. In vain because they opened fire on the youngsters mercilessly. I managed to dodge the bullets and be saved, but, alas, not so the children nor the jeep, which was riddled with bullets. I took the wounded kids in my hands, put them in the bullet-damaged jeep and drove directly to the Children's Hospital. There, I had a uniquely unpleasant experience. The doctor was afraid of reprisals against him and refused to operate on them. Then, with one of the children bleeding to death, I pulled out my gun, pressed it to his head and told him in Greek:

"Either you operate on this child or I execute you here and now!" He was stunned.

"Are you Greek? I thought you were American," he muttered.

"I am both a Greek and an American," I said. "So head to the operating room as fast as you can because these kids are bleeding heavily."

I still become rattled when I recall what happened at the hospital. However, my heart is further broken by what I discovered when I came to Greece in 1965, that is for the first time since the end of the war. A cousin of mine hosted us in the Halandri area. At noon one day, Peter cut his hand with a knife in the kitchen and I had to drive him to the Children's Hospital. While nurses were taking care of his wound, I asked the on-call physician if the Hospital retained medical response records from the war. I explained the reasons for my interest and added that I had served as an American officer in Greece. He returned holding a single cardboard box. I thought this could not be the only archive they had, but politely went through all the papers. I came across something I wished I never had seen. On the day following the operations on those children, "Chites" (members of the anticommunist and pro-royalist "Organization X") had walked into the Hospital and executed the kids in their beds. After that, I swore I would never return to Greece again. Peter and I returned to Halandri. I said nothing to anyone, not even to my wife. I felt such distress that I did not eat anything for days.

The second time my life was put in serious jeopardy was also during the "Dekemvriana" events in Athens. The Embassy was gravely alarmed by developments and, although Ambassador MacVeagh did not get along with me because I was the only American liaison with the guerrillas, I received orders from the OSS Chief of Mission in Greece, University Professor Gerald Else, whose office was in a Panepistimiou side street, to go to Liossa area and ask Orestis how things were. Orestis was a teacher from Euboea and the chief of the ELAS contingent on the outskirts of Athens. We had become acquainted when I fought in Macedonia and Thrace. I went to see him several times using a pass through Eleufsis that I learned very well because of my frequent visits to Orestis, who leading a force of 3000 men remained in his camp awaiting orders from ELAS.

One day, the firewood we used in our office for cooking was exhausted and Else ordered me to go out escorted by a private named Valonis, who knew Athens better than I did, to find firewood for the coming days, since it was clear that the situation was deteriorating. We went out, each driving his own jeep, with Valonis driving ahead of me, when suddenly, disobeying my orders to drive slowly, he accelerated and drove along a different street from the one we were supposed to take. Hearing the noise of car engines, the guerrillas, without having time to see the American flags, thought we were British and opened fire on us. Their bullets punctured not only the two front tires of my jeep, but also the fuel tanks tied to the side of the jeep. The fuel was seeping out from the holes. I swiftly jumped out of the jeep and ran away to save myself from the explosion which, however, miraculously did not happen. As soon as the ELAS guerrillas emerged from a nearby house, they heard me, with their eyes wide open in surprise, cussing them in very coarse Greek. I demanded they return to the house immediately and take cover before the British started shooting at them from the opposite side. If that happened, Valonis and I, being in the middle, would be the first to be killed. It was a good thing they heeded my advice. I was lucky to find two tires and was thus able to head to Liossa driving slowly via a route that was different to the one we usually took. I could speak to Orestis while Valonis gathered wood. It was the last time I saw Orestis.

The memories of that period continue to be very vivid in my mind and I often wake up from my sleep with a startled jump. This used to happen more often when I was younger, but they still come back and immerse me in deep sorrow. Instead of bringing joy and happiness to the Greek people for their ordeals, our entire struggle incurred new adventures, initially through the Civil War and later through the military dictatorship which we here in America tolerated and did nothing to avert. There were doubtless many voices in Congress, many Democrats who asked for the suspension of American aid to Greece to provoke the fall of the regime of the Colonels. But what prevailed were the voices of those who in the Cold War climate of that era saw Europe's security compromised by a Soviet rapprochement in its soft underbelly, that is, Greece and Turkey. This is the reason why the two countries continue to annually receive large economic aid after the war for their defense.

Too many people were crushed by their conscience. Accusations were concocted against innocent people who had fought against the German occupiers. Many were exiled, others were executed.

Greece was deprived of its best young men and women — deprived of people, in other words, with outstanding qualities and intellects that could indeed put the country on the road of progress. Within only five years after the war, the other European countries managed to put their economies back on their feet and created a uniform market for coal and steel that ultimately led to the creation of the European Communities. During the same time, however, Greece continued to be torn asunder by civil war, which was the fault of both the British and the King. I will never stop saying this. It has been, and will continue to be, my strong belief for as long as I live because I lived through the events that transpired from within. What was most unfair was that those who were left behind to govern the country were those who left it in the lurch as soon as the occupiers entered Greece in conjunction with those who departed as the occupiers invaded Greece. Also, those who remained in the country chose to live in peace and completely uninvolved in the war that was waged in the cities and up in the mountains.

All of us who, in our enthusiasm, rushed to enlist in the American military to offer our services to the struggle given by both our countries also paid a dear price. We left behind our settled way of life, our jobs and our families without an eye toward any sort of reward, spurred on only by genuine and innocent love. We felt equally grateful both to our birthplace and to our second country which enabled us to lead a better life.

And this is something for which I paid a high price. But I do not regret it, no matter how callously and mercilessly I was persecuted.

I speak for myself and refer to my own troubles which I could never have imagined I would endure after returning to America.

The honors extended to me were followed by interrogations and social marginalization, damage to my work and finances, to a point that my family faced issues of survival.

```
IN REPLY REFER TO:          WAR DEPARTMENT
                      THE ADJUTANT GENERAL'S OFFICE
                          WASHINGTON 25, D. C.
                                                    3 0 JUN 1947


        SUBJECT:  Commission in the Army of the United States.

        TO:       Officers who served in World War II.



            1.  The Secretary of War has directed me to issue a
        commission, in the highest rank attained, to each officer
        relieved from active duty after serving honorably in the
        Army of the United States during the recent war, who has not
        been issued a commission subsequent to being processed for
        relief from active duty.

            2.  The commission herewith does not constitute a new
        appointment but is formal evidence of the highest military
        rank you attained.  It is forwarded to you with the grateful
        thanks and deep appreciation of the War Department for your
        services.


        1 Incl                     EDWARD F. WITSELL
          Commission                Major General
                                    The Adjutant General



        FL-99
```

Georgiades receiving a military distinction from Major Edward Witsell, of the Office of Adjutant General (dd. January 30, 1947).

Let me start from the beginning. When I returned to America on October 16, 1945, I stayed in Washington for six weeks. I had to go through the long ordeal of submitting reports to the country's military authorities. Psychologically, I was still in a state of shock.

I came across numerous Greeks living in America who were involved in the war in various ways. Some, like me, had been recruited by the OSS. Some were not actively involved in the war but, when it was over, they participated in organizations whose mission was to send aid in various forms to cover the social welfare needs of Greeks who suffered in a country torn apart due to a triple occupation.

Alex in his uniform with Giorgos Vournas, a member of AHEPA. Vournas was also recruited by OSS, traveled to Cairo but was dismissed soon blamed to be the nephew of Roussos, a leading member of the Greek Communist Party.

Giorgos Vournas and Couvaras belonged in the first category. I came to know Vournas through AHEPA. I had met him earlier in Cairo, shortly before my departure for Adrianople. He did not stay in Cairo for long, as I learned later, but was unexpectedly asked to return to Washington. Probably the fact that he was the nephew of Roussos, a leading member of EAM then, and a brother of a member of KKE, the Communist Party of Greece, was to be blamed for what happened to him. Although an ocean separated Greece from the US, Greeks in America took their political passions to America with them. It was these same passions that divided the Greek people during the civil war.

Under those circumstances, Hellenism in America was marching along the pathways of division. On the one side were those who supported the Resistance and EAM and on the other side were the pro-royalists, the conservatives. The Greek-American press played a significant role in cultivating this division. Two large circulation papers were published in New York at that time: *Atlantis*, which belonged to the pro-royal camp, and *Ethnikos Kyrix*, which was EAM-leaning. There was also a third low-circulation newspaper, *To Vima*, but that was clearly pro-communist. An article published in *Atlantis* was the reason why I was placed in the eye of the storm and why the anti-communist hysteria broke out in America after the war.

Alex military salute during a ceremony at ELAS camp in Liossa, Athens. The photo was surreptitiously taken and used against him after the war accused as pro-communist.

That article claimed that ELAS collaborated with the Bulgarians, which resulted in well-known atrocities in Evros, for which Odysseus was to be blamed exclusively. I was infuriated and wrote a letter to the editor of the newspaper, whose name was Vlastos. He did not publish it and I had to write for a second time detailing what the real story was. Again, he did not publish it. However, the other two newspapers did.

Unfortunately for me, one of EAM leading members, Costas Karagiorgis, happened to be in America at that time. When he returned to Greece, he had the letter published in *Rizospastis*, the KKE newspaper, which was illegally printed. From that moment onward, my entire life changed. I was labeled a communist and people would jeer at me wherever I went to make a speech in large American cities, no matter if I wore the uniform of the US Armed Forces. My efforts to calm the political passions and help build national conciliation, at least among Greek-Americans, came to nothing. I tried in vain to impress upon them that the Greek people back home needed clothing, food and medicine for their survival, and we, as patriots, had to rise to the occasion.

An important Greek-American, who had earned a PhD in Chemistry, Nikos Charonis, who happened to be in Washington, then immediately espoused my initiative to send aid to the Greeks who were persecuted due to their participation in the Resistance. He joined Couvaras and myself in organizing what we called "American Relief for Greek Democracy," the ARGD. Charonis was appointed as the Chairperson of ARGD, alternating with war correspondent Robert Saint John. There were three Chairpersons, Frank Gevarsi, a war correspondent, a well-known Greek-American artist Vassos, who was recruited by the OSS, and I. Costas Couvaras was the secretary of the Organization.

Our big break came when we announced that the widow of President Roosevelt and Pulitzer-award winner *NY Post* journalist Leland Stowe were to be the Organization's big sponsors. The benefit from the participation of these two personalities was much higher than their actual economic contribution because they had major resonance in contemporary American society. As a result of the immense impact of the ARDG, the infamous HUAC (House Un-American Committee) began an investigation on the activities of communist cells in America. We were all instantly dubbed fellow-travelers. Mrs. Roosevelt resigned, apparently following pressure exerted on her, and eight months later we were forced to disband the organization. Stowe stayed by our side to the end. Charonis was persecuted more than anyone else. He died in 1961, after having gone through a great deal of suffering. I was gravely saddened. The good thing was that, during that brief period, we were able to gather 60 thousand dollars and clothing, all of which we sent back to Greece. Nonetheless, we did not give up. After President Roosevelt's death, America, one may argue, changed. It was no longer the land of democracy, freedom and ideals we had come to know. Yet, we, as its true sons, who had loved it as our second homeland, had not changed. We were looking for new ways and means to help Greece.

Charonis and I agreed that the issue that mattered most to the Greek people at that moment, if they were to survive, was food. And so, we gave it priority. Our first concern, therefore, were efforts to advance livestock breeding. Nikos knew that the Wallace brothers owned a huge farm at Doylestown, a little outside of Philadelphia, where they raised a very advanced breed of chicken that could produce up to 200 eggs per year. We asked one of Nikos' nephews in Greece to come to America and be trained at the Wallace Farm and we all went there. We managed to set up an enterprise in record time.

That, however, was not enough. Children in Greece had no milk. Greeks slaughtered the livestock the Germans had not confiscated to survive as hunger decimated them. At the same time, working animals, like horses, mules and donkeys, were in scarcity. The Germans had exterminated them all.

The question was how to transport all these across the Atlantic. Then, the Skouras Brothers came to my mind. They were successful Greek entrepreneurs in the realm of entertainment and had very powerful acquaintances and connections. I knew George Skouras personally. They were three brothers and George was my friend. All three Skouras brothers loved Greece and had never once declined to help the country. I spoke to George and he immediately arranged transportation through ship-owners friends of his family. Operation "Animals for Greece" proved successful.

One full year passed with me doing these sorts of chores. In the meantime, I was flat broke. I had to make up my mind what to do with my work and life from here on.

Skouras Theatres Corporation

PARAMOUNT BUILDING
1501 BROADWAY
NEW YORK

EXECUTIVE OFFICES

June 21, 1946

Mr. Alex Georgiades
220 Oakland Avenue
Pittsburgh, Pa.

My dear Alex:

They all say that there is no better word in the American
language to express one's gratitude to another than a single
thank you. It is exactly this that I want to transmit to
you for all the help and co-operation that I have received
from you and the committee in your town interested in the
Greek War Relief's GIVE AN ANIMAL TO GREECE campaign. Nation-
ally, this drive is a phenomenal success and that is due to
the altruistic and patriotic efforts of people like you and
your fellow townsfolks who helped make it a success.

Please give each one who worked or is working on this prac-
tical program my sincere thanks for being so kind and helpful to me while in your hospitable town.

As a last thought, I wish to suggest that if at any time you
visit New York City please call me. I would be most anxious
to talk with you and to thank you again personally.

Sincerely yours,

Nick John Matsoukas

Thank You letter sent to Georgiades from the Skouras Bros
Entertainment Enterprises for his participation in the "You, Too, Can
Gift an Animal to Greece" campaign.

At first, I turned down the proposal to work for the CIA, the
successor of the OSS after it was dismantled, despite the tantalizing offer
they made. It seems my refusal also weighed in the persecution I suffered
later. I should acknowledge I initially met with them out of curiosity, to
see what kind of work I could do for them. I was escorted into an office

where a heavy-set middle-aged woman told me I would need to pretend to be an owner of a ceramics factory on the Turkish coast. However, I was told that my reports should not report developments as they occurred, but they would need to be contrived on the basis of guidelines given to me. I refused and walked out. Many years later, recalling how the CIA worked, I came to realize why we made a mess of things in many places of the world.

When I left America to go to war, I could not have known if I would ever be able to return to my small lighting business and my two employees. I left without asking for compensation. Money was never an issue for me. My two superior officers in the Army were aware of that and I am confident they have submitted reports for their archives. They must have also reported the reason why they sacked Amoss from Cairo when they discovered he had mismanaged the money sent to him. What a disgrace. It is true I handled large amounts of money, both dollars and gold sovereigns. This money was to suborn Turkish officers; to buy food and medicine for the guerrillas; to make transfers in their names when they had to purchase various necessities; to compensate couriers; to pay the rent of my house which served also as my headquarters; to buy gasoline for the car I used to complete various assignments; and for so many other things that had to be accomplished as I deemed requisite. I briefed the Cairo Headquarters of all of my expenditures in detail.

It was comical that, when I returned to America, I needed to repurchase my own enterprise from the employees to whom I had sold it for one dollar. I was drowning in debt from the loans I had to take out to replace the old equipment which was in disrepair due to lack of maintenance. I sacked both employees and restarted the enterprise from scratch. I hired a designer, Maria Grazziani of Italian origin, who later became my wife and who also worked as my secretary and accountant. She received customer orders, designed electrical fixtures and made all payments to suppliers. She was a very talented and astute woman who had studied graphic arts at a local college in Pittsburgh.

In order to have more space where we could both work and live, we relocated to a place about 12 miles outside the city in a farm situated in the woods. The farm proved to be an ideal place for us and the three children we already had, as they grew up in the clean air of the countryside.

One of my employees was a Greek-American from Crete named Christianakis, a chemist by profession. He was introduced to me by Charonis when the latter was doing research on a new kind of wood through which he intended to hit the American market running. Neither of us was aware of that young man's character, who proved to have extreme conservative views and who eventually became an informer against us. Here, I must re-emphasize that the America of my era, the America we knew under the enlightened rule of President Roosevelt, is completely different from the country we know today. Back then, McCarthy's star ruled over the country. It was the worst period the US ever lived through. Half of America informed on the other half. It was the first and only time when a climate of hysteria, fear and suspicion poisoned the souls of the American people, who had been nurtured in the virtues of democracy, freedom of speech and thought and the philosophy of classical Greece in the manner taught by our ancient ancestors.

The role of Christianakis was unmasked through a chance event. A student from the Egyptian city of Ismaïlia, named Pete Psiroukis, was in our employment then. He was a good lad with a penchant for studies who I brought with me when I returned from Cairo. I undertook to pay his tuition fees and in exchange he worked in my enterprise. One morning, while cleaning our work space, he found in the waste bin a carbon copy of a letter that Christianakis addressed to the FBI. You can't even imagine what he alleged about me. He claimed I was a Bolshevik sympathizer who organized meetings of like-minded people in my home, that we all schemed to proselytize new members for the organization and that I received money from abroad to further these goals. The letter included loads of ridiculous and pathetic calumnies that I cannot even remember after so many years.

I nearly went crazy. I immediately asked to see him and showed the letter to his face, demanding that he explain himself. The more he remained speechless looking at his toes with his head bent forward, the angrier I became. What a snake in the grass! I cussed at him with words I had never used for anyone in the past, paid him outstanding wages, so he had nothing against me, and kicked him out.

I must admit that I was really upset by this incident. I could not condone such a shameless lie. It was accurate that we used to have gatherings with lots of friends, including Charonis, at the farm and, since the Presidential election of 1948 was approaching, we had more meetings that gradually became noisier as we handled print material to support the candidacy of Henry Wallace, 33rd Vice President of the US, under the Roosevelt Presidency, who lost the nomination of the Democratic Party because of his views favoring a mild policy towards the Soviet Union. The Democrats carried the elections thanks to Hoover's support and in the end, Wallace came up fourth with his Progressive Party. I could never believe that publicly supporting an American candidate with moderate views like Wallace could be the sole reason for anyone to make such heavy charges against me. As a matter of course, Charonis was also implicated.

The next rough blow came through a registered letter from the Army containing an open sewer of accusations against me. I kept the letter in my hands for a long time, greatly astonished. Maria asked me what the letter said, but I thought I should not tell her, knowing she would become distraught. I understood how wrong I was a few days later when we returned home and saw the babysitter of our daughter Thalia — our boys had not yet been born — tied on a chair with her hands in the back and the baby sobbing inconsolably in her playpen. We were nearly driven crazy. We untied her hands and she told us that police agents had tied her in the chair. They asked her to give them information about hidden weapons, asking her if she had noticed me using a radio transmitter, and they also wanted to know if I received checks with funds from overseas. The poor woman seemed to be terrified and the only thing she wanted was for us to find a new babysitter. She no longer wished to be close to us, had no complaints whatsoever from us, but she was scared for herself and her family.

We walked out with her to say goodbye and then noticed that the warehouse door was open. We went in and it was a total mess. It had been searched and everything was turned upside down. The same was true of the basement, the rest of the house and even the farm's chicken coop.

I was infuriated. And what I saw was just the beginning. It goes without saying that I did not reply to the letter the Army sent me. I sent a message, though, to the FBI. I let them know that from now on they should check with me personally whenever they needed information and not annoy and intimidate people who knew nothing and were not to be faulted for anything.

Shortly afterwards, an auditor from the Department of the Treasury paid a visit to my house. He wanted to learn why I had not declared a gun I brought with me when I came back to America after the end of the war.

CONFIDENTIAL

DEPARTMENT OF THE ARMY
OFFICE OF THE ADJUTANT GENERAL
WASHINGTON 25, D. C.

IN REPLY REFER TO

MF/eds

AGPR-F 201 Georgiades, Alexander M.　　　　　31 May 1951
01704215 (31 May 51)

SUBJECT:　Allegations

TO:　　　Captain Alexander M. Georgiades, AUS
　　　　　220 Oakland Avenue
　　　　　Pittsburgh 13, Pennsylvania

　　1.　The following allegations are on file in the Department of the
Army:

　　　　a.　In November 1940, you had as witnesses to your naturalization
two individuals who have been active in Communist affairs.

　　　　b.　You were the founder of a Communist movement among individuals
of Greek nationality and actively preached Communism. You favored the
Communist system of government and were recognized as the leader of the
pro-Communist faction in a Greek community.

　　　　c.　You were furnished a large sum of money by leaders of the Communist movement in Greece to be used to further the cause of Communism among
Greeks in the United States.

　　　　d.　At the time the Greek-Turkish Aid Bill was being considered by
the United States Congress, you took a personal interest in the matter, and
made a number of public speeches in which you indicated adherence to the
Communist Party line by:

　　　　　　(1) Stating in May 1947, that there was nothing to fear from
　　　　　　　　Communism; that you had worked with the Communists, lived
　　　　　　　　and slept with them in Greece; and that those who live by
　　　　　　　　the free enterprise system should not oppose Communism if
　　　　　　　　the other system can give people a better way of life.

　　　　　　(2) Predicting that if there was an election in Greece at that
　　　　　　　　time (1947), the country would elect a "Peoples' Government."

　　　　　　(3) Asserting that if the United States wanted to furnish aid to
　　　　　　　　the Greek people, such aid should be in the form of food,
　　　　　　　　clothing and other items to raise economic standards; that
　　　　　　　　there was no reason to fear Communism in Greece, and there-
　　　　　　　　fore this country should not send military supplies, but only

CONFIDENTIAL

Confidential document dd. May 31, 1951, from the Office of Adjutant
General listing a variety of accusations against Georgiades which he
is called upon to answer, to which he never did because they were
baseless. That was the era marked by the rise of McCarthy's in America
and the onset of the Cold War for all humanity.

"A weapon?" I asked.

"Yes, a weapon," he retorted.

"What kind of weapon?" I asked.

"You tell me," he answered in a totally sarcastic tone.

Then, I remembered that, while I was in Cairo, I had sent, via military pouch, a semi-automatic German Schmeisser, given to me as a token by Aris and Konstandaras when I left the Evros area. Naturally, I had completely forgotten about it because, when I traveled to Chicago to give one of my lectures, Jim Charakas, who had seen me mailing it from Cairo, said he wanted to have it.

He wanted to give it to Raymond Ickes — son of Harold Ickes, the Interior Secretary in the Roosevelt Administration. At least, that is what Charakas told me. And I sent the weapon to him. To verify what I was saying, I gave the auditor Charakas' address and telephone numbers in Chicago.

I never did learn if he called him. I warned Charakas to be mindful, and he did his best to allay my fears. His behavior, nonetheless, seemed bizarre to me. I did not ever reveal my afterthoughts and, though we continue to talk to each other to date, I still wonder about the role he played in this story and if he did in fact give the weapon to Ickes' son.

Not only did things fail to improve after this, but in fact they became far worse.

The FBI started paying me successive uncalled-for visits. From those visits, I recollect a specific one, during which two very courteous FBI agents stayed in my office over two hours. They asked me lots of questions, most of which were unimportant. When the interrogation was over, they could not conceal their embarrassment. They commended both my action during the war and my decorations, which they knew about, apparently, after having read classified files from military authorities.

"Since you are aware of all these things, why did you come here to ask me all that nonsense?" I asked them.

"We are obliged to do so, Mr. Georgiades. We could not do otherwise from the moment individuals whom you thought of as your friends made accusations against you."

Their reply resounded like a thunderclap in my ears.

On a different occasion, they telephoned and requested me to join them at a restaurant, which was on the floor above a friend's office, where they used to have lunch. They waited for me at the entrance of the restaurant and we did not go in. They produced a picture of a man, thought to be a hard-line communist, who was perceived a serious national threat, and asked me if I knew him. Without even looking at the picture, I told them that, if I knew someone was a national threat, I would turn him in myself.

"If you're looking for an informant, sorry," I said. "Search for them elsewhere." And then I walked — no, almost ran — away.

I was overwhelmed by both wrath and sorrow and felt my body burning, as if I had a high fever. I was so dismayed. So many sacrifices in the war seemed to have been wasted. I found myself counting the times my life was saved at the last moment, as if by a miracle. And what was the result? It seemed I had survived merely to be disgraced like this — and in my own homeland which had twice awarded me: first by making me a Captain in the American Army, and second through the Legion of Merit.

The FBI did not show up again. I never learned why. The Treasury Department, however, kept up the psychological pressure against me. For three consecutive years, they tossed my accounting office, going over all of our papers with a fine-tooth comb, but without, in the end, finding any irregularities at all. On the contrary, they reimbursed us 34 dollars.

The financial loss we suffered because of the war became worse because we kept losing customers. I think of good customers who had trusted us for years, such as the Budweiser and Schlitz breweries, with whom we had pre-war agreements. One after another, contracts they had with us were rescinded — and even worse than that, they took away Maria's designs. A customer, who also happened to be a good friend, confessed to me that he was approached by agents who suggested that, for his own good, he should refrain from consorting with me. I could not believe it! That was unprecedented.

I visited more of our customers afterwards and they told me the same things. Yet, no one seemed willing to testify in court. Such was the terror that the FBI had spread among our society. I was beside myself. Had it not been for my family, for whom I cared so much and for whom I felt responsible, who knows what I could have done trying to vindicate myself. Having lost major customers who accounted for most of our income, we dealt with small orders and our finances continued to deteriorate. We paid back our bank loans with great difficulty. We were able to offer our children milk and food thanks to our own farm-produced goats, eggs and groceries.

Almost two decades went by before things were under control in a way. But by then I was nearing retirement age. At that moment, I took the bold step to return to Greece with my family. I rented a very nice house at the Polydrosso area and enrolled my children at the American College. We had a difficult time adjusting to the prevailing living conditions — particularly so for the children — and one year later we felt compelled to return to America.

During the time we lived in Greece, I was able to free myself from many demons that had oppressed me for years. I met friends and foes whom I had known from the years of the Resistance. And there, in unassuming coffee houses, I talked with many of them and reconciled with them. At the end of the day, we are only human and all have weaknesses and virtues. Life was an uphill battle.

I hope, after my death, that my children will be able to figure it all out and clear my name from the mud and muck thrown at me. My eldest son, Peter, is a young lawyer and knows how to handle such things. His initial effort to obtain the military records failed. He was told they got burned in a fire at Saint Louis. The FBI files are still classified. One day, they will be released and the distress and the woes which stifled us during those difficult years will come to the fore.

To questions of whether I regret my actions, and if, after all that I went though, I would again do things required of me by duty, my response is none other than: I would do exactly what my grandfathers and my father taught me. There is no love greater nor purer than the love one feels for one's homeland. I was blessed by God to have two homelands and I loved both of them equally! First, the homeland that brought me to life and, second, the homeland that breathed new life into me.

Greece and America!

Pittsburgh, 1974

Georgiades family in 1970's at Pittsburgh. Alex with his wife Maria and two of his children Thalia and Aristotle. Peter, his elder son is the photographer.

Sources

<u>Archival Sources</u>

Hellenic Ministry of Foreign Affairs, Diplomatic and Historical Archives, Athens, Greece.

National Archives and Records Administration, Record Group 226, Records of the Office of Strategic Services, Washington, D.C.

<u>Bibliograpy</u>

Vangelis Kassapis, *Στον κόρφο της Γκύμπρενας: Χρονικό της Εθνικής Αντίστασης στον Έβρο* [At the Gymbrenas Grove: Chronicle of the National Resistance in Evros], two volumes, (Komotini: 1995).

Patrick O'Donnell, *Operatives, Spies, and Saboteurs: The Unknown Story of the Men and Women of World War II's OSS* (New York: Free Press, August 2006).

Richard Harris Smith, *OSS: The Secret History of America's First Central Intelligence Agency* (Connecticut: Lyons Press, 2005).

Barry Rubin, *Istanbul Intrigues* (Istanbul: Pharos Books, 2002).

Susan Heuck Allen, *Classical Spies: American Archaeologists with the OSS in World War II, Greece* (Ann Arbor, MI: University Michigan Press, 2011).

Kyriakos Nalmpantis, *Time on the Mountain: The Office of Strategic Services in Axis-Occupied Greece, 1943-44* (Kent, OH: Dissertation, Kent State University, 2010).

Elias Vlanton, Documents: The OSS and Greek Americans (*Journal of the Hellenic Diaspora* 9:31–84, Spring 1982).

Angeliki Laiou, *Αντάρτες και Συμμαχικές Αποστολές στον γερμανοκρατούμενο Έβρο. Η μαρτυρία του Αλέκου Γεωργιάδη* [Guerilla and Allied Missions in German-Occupied Evros. The Testimony of Alekos Georgiades.] Proceedings of the International Historical Congress, "Greece, 1936-1944: Dictatorship, Occupation, and Resistance," Athens, Educational Institute of ATE, 1989.

Dekemvriana (December Events): Clashes fought during and after WWII in Athens, from December 3, 1944 to January 11, 1945, spread all over Greece, known as the Greek Civil War.

EAM (National Liberation Front/ **E**thniko **A**peleftherotiko **M**etopo)

EDES (**E**thnikos **D**imokratikos **E**llinikos **S**yndesmos / National Republican Greek League)

ELAS (Hellenic Popular Liberative Army / **E**llinikos **L**aikos **A**peleftherotikos **S**tratos)

EPON (**E**niaia **P**anhellinia **O**rganosi **N**eon/ United Panhellenic Organization of Youth)

KKE (Communist Party of Greece / **K**ommounistiko **K**omma **E**lladas)

OPLA (Organization for the Protection of Popular Fighters/ **O**rganosi **P**rostasias **L**aikon **A**goniston)

OSS (Office of Strategic Services)

PEEA (Political Committee of Ethnic Liberation/ **P**olitiki **E**pitropi **E**thnikis **A**peleftherosis)

SNOF (**S**lavic-Macedonian **N**ational **F**ront)

UNRRA (United Nations Relief and Rehabilitation Administration)

9 789355 463746